SPECIAL MESSAGE TO READERS

This book is published by

THE ULVERSCROFT FOUNDATION

a registered charity in the U.K., No. 264873

The Foundation was established in 1974 to provide funds to help towards research, diagnosis and treatment of eye diseases. Below are a few examples of contributions made by THE ULVERSCROFT FOUNDATION:

A new Children's Assessment Unit at Moorfield's Hospital, London.

•

Twin operating theatres at the Western Ophthalmic Hospital, London.

•

The Frederick Thorpe Ulverscroft Chair of Ophthalmology at the University of Leicester.

•

Eye Laser equipment to various eye hospitals.

If you would like to help further the work of the Foundation by making a donation or leaving a legacy, every contribution, no matter how small, is received with gratitude. Please write for details to:

THE ULVERSCROFT FOUNDATION,
The Green, Bradgate Road, Anstey,
Leicester LE7 7FU. England

Telephone: (0533)364325

Love is
a time of enchantment:
in it all days are fair and all fields
green. Youth is blest by it,
old age made benign:
the eyes of love see
roses blooming in December,
and sunshine through rain. Verily
is the time of true-love
a time of enchantment — and
Oh! how eager is woman
to be bewitched!

SISTER TO JANE

Lady Katherine, beautiful and wayward sister to Lady Jane Grey, was passionately attached to Ned Hertford and desired only to be his wife. Brought up to be Royal Princesses, the wishes of Katherine and Jane were completely disregarded by their ambitious parents, and they found themselves pawns in the ruthless game for political power which eventually led to Jane's execution and meant a life of deceit and intrigue for Katherine.

BEATRICE MAY

SISTER TO JANE

The Story of Lady Katharine Grey

Complete and Unabridged

ULVERSCROFT
Leicester

First published in Great Britain in 1983 by
Robert Hale Limited
London

First Large Print Edition
published August 1992

British Library CIP Data

May, Beatrice
Sister to Jane.—Large print ed.—
Ulverscroft large print series: romance
I. Title
823.914 [F]

ISBN 0–7089–2696–7

Published by
F. A. Thorpe (Publishing) Ltd.
Anstey, Leicestershire

Set by Words & Graphics Ltd.
Anstey, Leicestershire
Printed and bound in Great Britain by
T. J. Press (Padstow) Ltd., Padstow, Cornwall

Brightness falls from the air,
Queens have died young and fair . . .
(Thomas Nashe)

1

LADY Katherine Grey stifled a yawn and wriggled uncomfortably in her long, brocaded bridesmaid's gown. She was hot and weary from the task of holding the bride's train, for the ceremony had been a long one. The great hall of her father's house was crowded with richly dressed ladies and gentlemen, talking, laughing, dancing and pressing round the bride and her groom. The girl weaved her way round them, edging stealthily behind a wide farthingale to avoid the censure of her mother, the Duchess of Suffolk, and at last escaped into the fresh air.

She paused and looked back at the great house. It was alive with light and colour and movement. This was what her mother loved more than anything; gaiety and parties, music and dancing, with herself the gracious doyen, preening herself but ruling with a rod of iron. She had needed little persuasion to act hostess at the wedding of her great friend, Bess Hardwick, now Mistress Saintlow.

It was a still, moonlit night, and Katherine lifted her long petticoats and ran across the dewy grass, exulting in her liberty. An owl hooted behind her, and she stood still, waiting, hoping. Was it really an owl, or was it — ? Ah! She shivered with delight as a pair of hands was clapped over her eyes, blindfolding her.

"What means this?" a voice demanded sternly. "Running away? Deserting your post? What behaviour is this for an attendant of the bride? Have you no decorum, child?"

"Let me go, Ned!" Katherine cried, tugging at his hands, but the more she pulled, the firmer was she imprisoned.

"A kiss, sweet little Kate. Give me a kiss and you shall go free," bargained the lad.

"Very well," the girl answered meekly, no longer struggling.

The young man released his pressure over her eyes. As fleet as a hare, she had gone, laughing as she ran from him. He followed and quickly caught up with her and grabbed her flowing skirt. She stumbled and would have fallen but for his arms about her. She laughed, and panted breathlessly, her red lips parted. The boy bent his head and kissed her on her mouth, and she returned his kiss, warmly and sweetly. They stood close together in the moonlit garden, until the young man broke the spell with an incredulous laugh.

"By my faith, Kate," he said, "who taught you to kiss? I thought you were but a child."

"I'm twelve years old," she answered.

He could feel her heart beating against him, and he pushed her away from him, gently.

"Come, little Kate," he said, "let us go back."

"It's so lovely out here. Don't let's go in yet. Let us walk a little. Shall I show you my new pony?"

What the crowded, noisy mansion was to the Duchess of Suffolk, the stable, redolent with animal ordure and sweet hay, was to Lady Katherine. As she entered, her spaniels leaped to greet her with moist tongues and wagging tails;

her pony whinnied, and in a far corner a monkey swung excitedly and rattled the bars of its roomy cage.

"He goes like the wind," Katherine said, stroking the pony's nose. "Shall we go riding?"

"At this late hour?"

"Why not? The moon is shining bright as daylight. I would love to ride."

The boy laughed. She was a wild pretty creature, he thought, like a little animal herself. Yes, that was it, like a little wild fawn. He felt a fierce desire to kiss her again, to tumble her on to the sweet-smelling hay which was piled in a corner of the stable. But she, it seemed, had thoughts only for her pony now.

"Shall we, Ned?" she was pleading. "Shall we go riding in the moonlight?"

"Oh, very well," he agreed. "I will have our mounts saddled, while you exchange that dainty dress for your riding habit. But be quick, and don't let your mother catch you, or there will be the devil to pay."

"Alas, 'tis true!" she agreed. "A sound box on the ears, or perhaps a beating, will be my lot if I am caught."

"And well-deserved, I have no doubt," he threw after her as she hurried away excitedly.

Within ten minutes they were both mounted and trotting away from the garden pleasance to the wilder part of Bradgate estate, where bracken covered the rough, rocky land, and squirrels hid in tall trees.

"Hist!" cried Lord Hertford, suddenly reining in his horse.

"What is it?" asked Katherine. "I heard nothing."

Ned pointed with his whip towards a clump of ferns, out of which a pair of bright eyes glittered evilly.

"What is it?" the girl whispered.

A creature leapt from the undergrowth and bounded away. Ned drew his dagger, a bejewelled, slender blade, more for ornament than use, and gave chase. The animal dashed across open country, followed by the two horses, and ran to cover in a dark cavern, hewn out of rock. Lord Hertford dismounted and rushed into the cave, his dagger raised above his head. The beast crouched motionless, its fanged mouth open, ready to spring, and the young man stopped, petrified with sudden fear, cursing the folly which had led him to dismount and follow the creature into the cave.

A heavy rock hurtled past Ned and crashed against the creature's head. It staggered, then sank back upon its haunches and expired at once, soundlessly.

"God's death!" exclaimed the youth, laughing with relief and excitement. "Did you throw that, Kate? You've killed him. You've killed the brute and saved my life."

"What is it, Ned?" Katherine asked, shuddering as she looked at the dead animal, its eyes glazed, its long tongue lolling out of its mouth.

"It's a wolf. I wouldn't have had a chance against him with this toy of a dagger. I must have been crazed to follow him into the cave."

"A wolf! But I thought they had all been killed off, long since. I never saw one before."

"They are very rare now. I've never heard of one being seen in Bradgate Park before."

"It looks malevolent still, even in death," shuddered Katherine.

"I would have been torn to pieces by now, but for your good aim, sweet Kate."

"Come away. Let's go back to the house." Now that the danger was over, Kate was trembling violently.

"We'll take him with us. I warrant he'll be more of an attraction than the bride herself."

Ned slung the wolf over his saddle with Katherine's protesting help and they trotted soberly back. Although it was well past midnight the wedding party showed no signs of breaking up, and when Katherine and Ned entered the great hall, the guests were being merrily entertained by a company of morris men.

The Duke and Duchess of Suffolk were sitting with the bride and bridegroom and some of their guests on a raised dais at the end of the hall. Katherine and Ned began to relate their adventure to them, excitedly.

"You killed a wolf? But that is not possible, my child. There are no wolves at Bradgate."

Lady Katherine's father was gently sceptical, her mother more harshly so.

"Do not tell us such falsehoods," she cried, and forgetful of the presence of her guests, she struck Katherine such a sharp blow on the cheek with her folded fan, that it left a crimson weal across the girl's face.

"It is true, madam," said Katherine, more quietly now, her spirits quenched.

"And what have you done with this fearsome beast?" asked the Duchess, turning to Lord Hertford.

"I threw it across my saddle and brought it back. Come outside and I will show it to you."

"Let us go and inspect it," said the Duke of Suffolk.

Ned and Katherine led the way followed by all the wedding guests, curious to know what was going on. The morris dancers were left jigging to an empty hall.

"There!" cried Ned, triumphantly, pointing to the limp body sprawled in the courtyard.

Amid cries of amazement, the dead wolf was inspected, prodded by the gentlemen, and shuddered over by the ladies. Lady Katherine's exploit in killing the beast was passed from mouth to mouth, losing nothing in the telling.

"Lady Katherine saved my life," Ned Hertford said, again and again.

It was a new experience for Katherine to be the centre of attention. She was a pretty child and high-spirited, but she was accustomed to being overshadowed by her intellectually brilliant, elder sister, Lady Jane. There were three sisters, Jane the scholar, Katherine who gave promise of great beauty, and little Mary, who was so small as to be accounted a dwarf. Their mother, Frances Brandon, Duchess of Suffolk, was cousin to the boy-king, Edward VI, her mother being old King Harry's sister Mary.

The three girls were being brought up like princesses, as befitted their closeness to the throne of England. Indeed, it was mooted that the Lady Jane would make a fitting wife for young King Edward, being of the same age. She was at present domiciled in London under the guardianship of Admiral Seymour, with whom her parents were conspiring to promote the match.

But this was undoubtedly Lady Katherine's night. When at last the bride and bridegroom had been escorted to the nuptial bed, with much laughter and coarse jests, and the wedding party was over, Katherine lay wakeful in her own bed, reliving every moment of her ride, the killing of the wolf and the kiss between her and handsome Lord Hertford. She was very, very happy.

At last she slept, and dreamed that she, and not Bess Hardwick, was the bride. Hand-in-hand with Ned Hertford, she was being escorted to the nuptial bed, followed by a noisy, laughing crowd. But suddenly their way was barred by a pack of wolves, open-mouthed, cruel fangs bared, slobbering tongues protruding.

She shrieked and awakened, and was relieved to find herself in bed. For a few moments she was confused, and the events of the previous night were mixed with her dream. Her mind cleared. Of course. The bride was Bess Hardwick, not herself But there had been a wolf and she had killed it, and Ned, Lord Hertford owed his life to her.

Lying in her bed, Katherine went over the events of the evening before. It had all begun in fun when Ned had chased her, as he had chased her many times. But this time, the chase had ended with a kiss. She closed her eyes and relived those moments of magic. He had been surprised. "Who taught you to kiss?" he had said. And she, too, had been surprised at herself. But it had happened so naturally, so inevitably. Ned and her. It was all so wonderful. And she had saved his life. She heard again the warmth in his voice as he had told the story of their adventure.

"Kate saved my life!" he had said, over and over again.

They had long been companions, had laughed and played together, while Jane, her brilliant elder sister would be deep in conversation with her cousin, the young king. The New Learning — always the New Learning, the Protestant faith, was what they discussed so earnestly. Indeed, they were well suited. But Edward was pale and delicate, not like handsome Lord Hertford. Jane was welcome to share the throne of England with her sickly cousin, but she, Katherine, would marry Ned Hertford.

Katherine stretched voluptuously in her bed, then, tossing the coverlet aside, she rose, and taking up a mirror studied her face intently. She was pleased with what she saw. Her red-gold curls framed a heart-shaped face with blue-green eyes. Yes, she was pretty. Jane could have her king, and she, Katherine, would be betrothed to Ned Hertford.

Mrs Ellen, their old nurse, entered the bedchamber and cut short Katherine's blissful reverie.

"Time to be dressed, my lady, or you will be late for prayers," she said, bustling about, "for it is close upon six o'clock."

"What think you of my Lord Hertford?" asked Katherine, as she was being hooked into a voluminous bell-shaped skirt of shimmering damask rose.

"A pretty boy, forsooth," replied Nurse Ellen, giving her young mistress a shrewd glance, "but he is not for you."

"And why not, pray?" asked Lady Katherine, tossing her head defiantly, but with a sudden feeling of apprehension. "Why not?"

Nurse Ellen was omniscient. Katherine had never known her to be wrong.

"Why not?" she repeated impatiently.

But the old nurse shut her lips tightly and would say no more.

Each day began with prayers and a reading from the Bible, conducted by the Dorsets' chaplain, Haddon, and attended by all the household. Breakfast followed, a meal of bread and meat, washed down by thin ale. The rest of the morning Katherine must spend with her tutor, Master Aylmer. Good Master Aylmer, so patient and gentle, would be waiting for her in the quiet schoolroom, while all about them would be bustle and colour and life. Many people were entertained at this great house at Bradgate, and the hall was generally crowded. There were hunts and gaming parties and dances, and sometimes priests from abroad came to consult with the mighty Duke of Suffolk, for he, too, professed great zeal for the New Learning.

Somewhere in that brilliant throng Ned Hertford would be, and Katherine sat and dreamed and longed for a sight of him.

"What ails you, my Lady Katherine?" asked her tutor with a sigh, observing her inattention. Truly, this one was difficult to teach, unlike her studious sister.

"Forgive me, Master Aylmer," pleaded Katherine, "I am weary after the excitement of Mistress Saintlow's wedding."

"Ah! Yes, of course. I will excuse you further study today," said her tutor, only too willing to release her.

So Katherine found herself free to wander at will.

Losing no time, she gathered up her skirts, and ran across the close-cropped grass, just as she had done the night before. This time she was not followed by Lord Hertford. The pleasance was deserted, for the Duke had taken his guests out hunting in the forest of Charnley, adjacent to the estate of Bradgate. But her pets were eager to greet her, and after caressing her spaniels, Katherine unlocked the door of her little chimpanzee's cage. He leaped upon her shoulder and covered her face with kisses.

"Beppo," cried Katherine, "I have been excused my lessons, so I have come to play with you. Shall we dance, Beppo?" and she twirled round rapidly, the little monkey clinging to her giddily.

"There, Beppo, did you like that? Now, listen to me, Beppo. I wish to ask you a question. How like you my Lord Hertford? Is he the most handsome gentleman of your acquaintance? Is he, Beppo? Is he? Yes, he is, he is, he is. Now listen to me. No, don't pull my hair. I have something to tell you. Last night, Beppo, do you recollect that we visited you at midnight, and then we rode out together? I saved my Lord Hertford's life. I killed a wolf. What do you think of that, eh? There, you don't care, do you Beppo? Never mind, let us take a walk together."

She gathered the little monkey into her arms and left the stable, followed by her spaniels, who jumped around her excitedly.

"Listen, Beppo! I hear horses. Surely the hunt is not returning already? Let us go to meet them."

It was not the hunt returning that Katherine met in the cobbled forecourt of the house, but a small cavalcade, escorting her sister Jane, who had been borne in a litter all the way from London.

"Jane, why Jane, my dear sister, we were not expecting you — "

The sisters embraced, which gave the little monkey a chance to scamper off. By the time he was recaptured and scolded, Jane, wearied after her long ride, had retired to her bedchamber, and Katherine saw no more of her that day.

The next morning Jane joined Katherine at her studies, much to Master Aylmer's delight. Katherine was curious to know the reason for her sister's unexpected return from London. Had Admiral Seymour, with whom she had been staying, been unable to effect the union of Jane with the young King Edward? It had been whispered that Admiral Seymour had paid a considerable sum of money to the Duke of Suffolk for the opportunity of arranging such a match, which would advance his favour with the young king, and thwart the plans of Seymour's brother, Lord Somerset, the Protector, of whom he was very jealous.

In truth, Admiral Seymour's ambition

had run away with him, to the extent that he had plotted to overthrow the Government, and seize the person of the king. The conspiracy was discovered, and Seymour was arrested and executed.

The king was to marry a foreign princess, it was whispered, and Lady Jane Grey had returned to her home a failure in the eyes of her parents, their ambitions for her thwarted.

Jane had nothing to say on the subject, but applied herself diligently to her studies, to the delight of Master Aylmer. She soon fell into the pattern of life she had followed before her sojourn in London, studying with Katherine in the mornings, reading or playing the lute after dinner, often joining in learned discussions with her father's visitors.

For Katherine the afternoons were a time of liberation, when she amused herself with her pets, exercised her pony, and was sometimes allowed to join the hunt. Of Lord Hertford she saw little, although he remained under her father's roof. Once she caught a glimpse of him flirting gaily with Lord Mewtas's pretty daughter, Arabella, and suffered violent pangs of jealousy.

But there were others only too willing and anxious to accompany Lady Katherine on her daily rides. One of these was the Earl of Pembroke's son, Herbert, a pale and languid youth, very much dominated by his father. Katherine tolerated his company, but found him a poor substitute for her beloved Ned Hertford.

Jane's return to Bradgate, so pleasing to her tutor, was such a disappointment and source of irritation to her mother, Lady Suffolk, that they were often at loggerheads. Her mother disapproved of Lady Jane's devotion to her books instead of joining in the gay social life enjoyed at Bradgate. She looked askance, too, at her daughter's quiet taste in dress. In accordance with her religious principles, Jane had set aside the gorgeous silks and velvets, tissues of gold and silver and gaudy jewels which her mother and those of similar exalted positions wore. Jane habitually wore a gown of black frieze, relieved only by a white barbette.

Katherine, too, found it difficult to

understand her sister's delight in learning.

"Books, books, always books," cried Katherine. "I am weary of reading. What is there in this Phaedo of Plato which interests you so much? You read it as though it were a merry tale of Boccaccio!"

"I am more happy when I am learning with dear Master Aylmer, who teaches us so gently and pleasantly than at any other time," declared Jane.

"It is true," sighed Katherine, "that mother and father are always sharp and severe with us."

"More so with me than with you. Mother requires absolute perfection in everything I do, whether I speak, keep silence, sit, stand, or go, eat, drink, be merry or sad, be sewing, playing, dancing or doing anything else."

"I know. If it is not done exactly as she orders it, there are pinches, nips and blows for us."

The sisters' lamentations were interrupted by a servant who curtsied and said to Jane, "Her Grace, your mother requires your presence at once, madam."

Jane looked at Katherine in dismay

then rose in instant obedience to the command.

"May the good Lord deliver you from our lady mother's pinches," cried Katherine flippantly.

But this time there was no reprimand for Jane. An invitation had been received by the Duke and Duchess of Suffolk and their daughter, Jane, to be present at court when Mary of Guise, the Queen Regent of Scotland was to be entertained by King Edward. The Duchess was delighted, Jane less so. She would much rather stay quietly at home with her books, than be involved in the extravagant splendour of royal entertainment.

"We have nothing fit to wear at court," purred the Duchess. "I must order new gowns to be made for us both without delay."

"Madam, I have given up wearing vain-glorious, gaudy apparel," said Jane firmly. "I will attend at court in my gown of black frieze."

"And bring shame upon us all with your poverty stricken air!" declared her mother, indignantly. "I cannot understand you, miss. There were cause for complaint if I kept you short of good clothes, but here am I, ready and anxious to dress you as befits a princess, and you are determined to robe yourself like a sewing-maid. Fie upon you! You will do as you are told."

So, in spite of her protests, a rich gown was made for Jane, of tinsel cloth of gold and velvet ornamental with golden parchment lace.

Jane burst into tears when she beheld it and fled to the old nurse, Mrs Ellen, to be comforted.

"What shall I do? What shall I do?" she sobbed.

"Do as her Grace, your mother, bids you," advised the old woman.

"And wear that — that frippery?"

"Marry, wear it, to be sure," was the firm answer.

So Lady Jane was dressed up in the height of the fashion. To finish off her costume she wore a most handsome pearl and ruby necklace, which had been sent to her by the king's half-sister, the Princess Mary.

Katherine came upon her sister Jane in their bedchamber, gazing into the mirror at the reflection of herself wearing the necklace. The red drops were drawn closely round her throat in the fashion of the moment, but they were distorted in the mirror by the flickering candlelight.

Katherine saw a look of horror on her sister's face.

"What ails you, Jane?" she began, then she, too, looked into the mirror and was appalled. The reflections of the red beads were lengthened, and looked for all the world like great drops of blood dripping down the Lady Jane's white neck.

"I will never wear it," Jane said, and tore the necklace off.

"It's beautiful," Katherine exclaimed, taking up the ruby collar, "and Princess Mary will be displeased if you don't wear her present."

"Then Princess Mary must be displeased. There are more weighty matters of dispute between Princess Mary and myself than the wearing of this bauble."

Katherine stared at her elder sister, and realized that this was a new Jane, invested with authority and a will of her own. Her sojourn in London had indeed changed her and developed her character.

Katherine was torn with jealousy when she discovered that Lord Hertford was to accompany her parents and Lady Jane to London. She poured out her heart to Mrs Ellen.

It was not fair. Why must it always be Jane who was chosen?Just because she was the eldest. Jane did not even want to go, did not appreciate her new, beautiful clothes and would much rather stay at home, studying with Master Aylmer.

"Don't take on so, my lady," her old nurse begged. "Your turn will come, never fear. Your pretty face will not go unnoticed for long. You will make a fine match, I'll be bound, and leave your sister far behind, for all her book learning."

Katherine refused to be comforted, and moped about disconsolately with her pets. Daily she rode to the cave where she had stoned the wolf. Did Ned ever think about that wonderful night? she wondered. Or was his life so full, so crowded, that it had slipped into the background, forgotten, as she would never forget it?

"Oh, Ned, come back, come back," she sighed. And come back he did. For when Lady Jane and her parents returned to Bradgate, Ned Hertford was with them.

Oh, it was wonderful, wonderful, to be sitting next to him for supper. He was so gay, so debonair, turning first to one sister and then the other, as he sat between them. Lady Dorset, the Duchess of Suffolk, too, was in her happiest mood, and very well disposed towards Lord Hertford, addressing him as 'her dear son'.

Tomorrow, Katherine thought, perhaps Ned will ride with me again.

But when tomorrow came, Ned was nowhere to be found, and Katherine must ride alone. Jane, no doubt, was deep in her books.

So, feeling a little lonely and disappointed, Katherine set out on her daily ride, through the pleasance into the wild part of the estate, where she could put her pony to the gallop, and shake off her depression.

To her surprise, she saw two riders in front of her, one of them Lady Jane, the other Lord Hertford.

Catching up with them she cried, "Good day to you, sister Jane, and my Lord Hertford."

"Good day, Katherine," replied Jane, "we were just speaking of you. It is well that you are here, for we have something to tell you."

"Something to tell me?" asked Katherine sharply. She had a sudden sensation of deep dismay as she saw the contented serenity of Jane's expression.

"Ned and I are to be betrothed."

"Betrothed? You and Ned? Oh no!"

"But, yes, indeed we are."

"But you are to marry King Edward, and be Queen of England."

"Edward is to marry a foreign princess."

"So our parents have decided that the son of the Lord Protector, the Duke of Somerset, will do for their eldest daughter, instead."

Lord Hertford looked at Katherine and looked hastily away. The consternation on her face was embarrassing and deeply troubling to him.

"It is true that our parents have arranged this match," Jane said gently, "but Ned and I will be very happy to be wed."

"I wish you well," Katherine said, then turning her horse's head, left them abruptly.

The entire household was assembled in the private chapel at Bradgate for the handfasting of Lady Jane and Lord Hertford. It was late summer, the day was overcast and thundery, and the crowded chapel hot and airless.

Seated between her mother and her little sister Mary, Katherine's head spun, and she felt sick with bitter jealousy of her sister Jane. Her eyes filled with tears as the couple stood with clasped hands before the chaplain and made their vows of constancy to each other. As they sealed their promises with a kiss, Lady Katherine gave a wild sob, and slid off her chair, senseless.

It was the heat, her elders said, and she was carried to her bedchamber. Nurse Ellen sat by her side, and gently bathed her head, while in the great hall a feast was held, with much gaiety and music, to celebrate the betrothal.

The Duchess of Suffolk was well content. Truly, she had been deeply disappointed that plans for her eldest daughter to marry the king had not materialized, but to be wedded to his cousin, the Protector's son, was surely the next best thing. For Lord Somerset, the Lord Protector, ruled the young king and directed him in all things. No man in all the land had more power than had Lord Somerset. And if the Duchess was content, so then was the Duke, for his lady wife ruled him in matters great and small. So the feasting and gaiety went on for many days, and many guests were entertained at Bradgate, following the handfasting of Lady Jane and Lord Hertford.

Only one person was seldom seen at these celebrations and that was Lady Katherine. She could not bear the sight of Lord Hertford, and avoided the company of her sister Jane, except for the time they must spend at their books with Master Aylmer. As often as she could she would slip away to the stables to be consoled by her beloved pets.

Therefore Katherine was quite unaware of the sudden change in the atmosphere, and of the rumours which began to circulate about the name of the King's Protector. She did not notice that Lord Hertford, Ned, her sister's betrothed, her mother's 'dear son' was suddenly not quite so dear, or that Lady Jane was worried and preoccupied.

Lady Katherine was weary of her books. Their tutor was engaged in an earnest disputation with Jane, and Katherine had been left to do some impossible Greek translation, unassisted. She felt rebellious, besides neglected, and acting on an impulse, got up quietly, and slipped away, out of doors.

Once out, in the warm sunshine, she picked up her skirts and ran, as always, across the grass to the stables. And here, booted and spurred, was Lord Hertford, about to mount and ride away.

"Ned!" she cried, and stood quite still.

"Kate! God's truth, but I am glad to

see you. Where do you get to, these days? I never set eyes on you. And now we are met, I must say goodbye to you at once."

"I — I have been busy with my books. But where are you going?"

"To London. I have had an urgent message from my mother. There is some trouble at court, between the Privy Council and my father. I don't understand what has happened, but my father has been arrested."

"Arrested?"

"Yes, he is in the Tower of London. I must go at once to see what is to be done to get his release."

"Oh, Ned! I am sorry."

"Thank you, Kate. Now I must be off. I've said farewell to your parents, but I've not seen Jane. I didn't want to disturb her at her books, and I'll soon be back. Will you tell her?"

"Yes, of course I will. And I hope your worry will soon be over and you'll return to us. Goodbye Ned."

She held out her hand, and he took it gently and raised it to his lips, then leaping into the saddle, he was off without a backward glance. Katherine watched him out of sight, then turned and slowly walked away.

Lord Hertford did not return to Bradgate. He was unable to effect the release of his father, who remained in the Tower over Christmas. Ned stayed in London with his mother.

The Duke and Duchess of Suffolk, with their three daughters set out on a round of visits, spending Christmas at Tylsey, with their kinsman, Lord Willoughby, who had assembled a most illustrious company of guests. Besides Princess Mary, the king's half-sister, the Duke and Duchess of Northumberland with their youngest son, Dudley, were present, and the Earl of Pembroke with his son, Lord Herbert. The young king, himself, was to have joined the party, but he had become ill, and was at Greenwich Palace, confined to his bed. None knew the nature of his illness.

To entertain them on Christmas Eve, Lord Oxford was persuaded to present his troupe of actors in a Nativity play. When the play ended, minstrels played for dancing, and the guests stepped in among the players. Guildford Dudley partnered Jane, and Herbert Pembroke took Katherine upon his arm for the galliard, their parents looking on approvingly.

In truth, Lord Herbert could outdance them all. He discarded the languid air and foppish ways which Katherine had deplored in him when they had ridden together at Bradgate. None tossed his partner more adroitly or higher in the air than did Lord Pemberton. Five quick steps, a beating of the feet together, a leap into the air and off again, the gentlemen all competing in tossing their partners the highest. The fun waxed fast and furious and the party did not break up until the early hours of the morning.

In spite of the late night, Christmas Day began early with the exchange of presents at the breakfast table. Gloves and embroidered sleeves, and ribbons and trinkets were exchanged, exhibited, admired and exclaimed upon.

No present had been received by Jane from Ned Hertford. Katherine wondered about his silence, and wondered how he was passing Christmas, and was his father still imprisoned in the Tower? Jane made no comment, but appeared to be her usual serene self.

The junketing, with masques and feasts and merrymaking, and with the Lord of Misrule turning all upside down, went on till Twelfth Night, after which the party moved on to another relative of the Suffolks, Lady Audley, at Saffron Walden.

Here, Mass was celebrated daily and the Host stood on the altar. This was in defiance of the law and against King Edward's wishes, for he was as ardent a Protestant as Lady Jane. She was scandalized, but contained her feelings until, one day, she was passing through the chapel with one of Mary's ladies-in-waiting, Lady Anne Wharton. That lady genuflected to the Host which was in its usual place upon the altar.

Lady Jane enquired if the Lady Mary was present in the chapel.

Lady Wharton said, "No."

"Why, then, do you curtsey?" asked Lady Jane.

"I curtsey to Him that made me," was the reply.

Jane said impatiently, "Nay, but did not the baker make him?"

"Christ said, 'This is my body and blood, which is shed for you,'" answered Lady Anne.

"He said 'Do this in remembrance of Me'. He is there in our thoughts and in our hearts. The Eucharist is a perpetual renewal of our faith, but the bread is still bread, and the wine is wine."

"You are misguided," said Lady Anne. "At the moment of consecration the substance of the bread is changed into the substance of the body of Christ and the substance of the wine into His blood."

This was the argument which was causing controversy up and down the whole country, and which was to cause the torture and death of many worthy and sincere people. And Lady Jane Grey, at this moment, had taken her first irrevocable step towards her doom.

Meanwhile, in London, false witnesses, bribed by the Duke of Northumberland testified against the Lord Protector, who was found guilty of high treason. Hc was accused of plotting to murder the Privy Council in order to install his own dictatorship. His lands were confiscated and he was sentenced to death. A few weeks later he was beheaded and divided into four quarters, dying irksomely, strangely and horribly. His son, Lord Hertford, was now without an inheritance, and his family in disgrace.

2

THE king's two uncles, the Seymours, having both been executed, the Duke of Northumberland was now the most powerful man in the land, nearest to the king, most influential in the Council. That he should condescend to join a hunting party at Bradgate, bringing with him his youngest son, the handsome Guildford Dudley, was a source of great satisfaction to the Duke and Duchess of Suffolk. Not so to Lady Jane, who found she had little in common with Guildford Dudley, though they were constantly thrown together. She found him arrogant, conceited, and worst of all, in Jane's eyes, empty-headed, in spite of the excellent education he had received, comparable with her own.

Jane was apprehensive, and when her studies were interrupted by a peremptory summons to her mother's solar, she went with some foreboding. Katherine saw no more of her sister that day, but when she retired for the night, to the chamber which they shared, she found Jane lying on her bed, her face tear-stained.

"What ails you, sister?" Katherine asked sympathetically.

"It is monstrous. I will not do it. I will not."

"Do what?"

"They say I am to marry that weakling, Guildford Dudley!"

"Marry Guildford Dudley?"

"So they say."

"Who says so? And how can you marry anybody but Ned? Were you not solemnly betrothed to him before the whole household?"

In spite of her genuine concern over Jane's distress, Katherine was unable to suppress a shock of joy. Her sister not to marry Ned Hertford? Could this be true?

Jane had begun to sob again.

"Come, Jane. Tell me all about it. What happened when you were summoned to mother's solar this morning?"

"They were all there — "

"Who?"

"Mother and father, and the Duke and

Duchess of Northumberland, and that odious son of theirs, Guildford. And they asked, nay commanded, me to accept the hand of Guildford Dudley in marriage."

"What did you reply?"

"I said no, and they asked why I refused so curtly. They were all displeased, but I answered that I was already solemnly betrothed to Lord Hertford."

"What answered they to that?"

"Father said the betrothal could be set aside. Indeed, he had no intention that I should marry Ned, now that his father had been executed, and his estates confiscated."

"Poor Ned."

"I said his changed circumstances made no difference to me, since I was already solemnly betrothed to him."

"And then?"

"Oh, a terrible scene! Mother shouting and threatening, and at last I was sent to my room, and here I am."

"Have you eaten?"

"No, but I am not hungry. I don't want anything to eat."

Katherine summoned Mrs Ellen, and with her help retired to bed without further conversation. There was no more to say, and indeed if she said anything to comfort her stricken sister, it would be sheer hypocrisy. She felt dizzy with the joy of knowing that Jane's betrothal to Ned was to be set aside. Surely, in spite of all her defiance, in the end her sister would have to obey their parents' wishes. She would not be allowed to marry Ned. But why this insistence on Jane's part that her betrothal could not be set aside? Was it that she would not break her promise to Ned because she loved him? Or simply that a promise was a promise? Many would be pleased to be coupled with Guildford Dudley, handsome and debonair as he was, and none so rich and important as his father. It was true that Guildford Dudley was no match for Jane intellectually, but then, neither was Ned Hertford, come to that. In truth, the king was the only one to really share Jane's interests, her commitment to the New Learning, and her delight in intellectual discourse. Katherine remembered how those two would sit together as little children, two heads bowed over one book. And yet, Jane had displayed no emotion, no regret, when it was realized that her parents' ambitions for her to be queen consort to the young king had come to nothing.

Was Jane in love with Ned Hertford? Did she feel the same way towards him as Katherine herself felt? And what of Ned? What were his true feelings towards Jane? Towards herself? The memory of that enchanted night came flooding back. Memory of the kiss they had exchanged. Surely, surely, Ned had meant it? Had felt for her, as she felt for him?

But even if Jane's betrothal were to be set aside, would Ned Hertford be allowed to pay court to her, Katherine? He was heir to a disgraced traitor, who had been executed, his estates confiscated. But Katherine was only the second daughter. It was on Jane her parents' hopes and ambitions were centred. Surely their second daughter's marriage would not be so important, and the disgrace of Lord Hertford's family would be soon forgotten. But their state of penury, would that be overlooked? The Duke and Duchess of Suffolk would find that harder to forgive.

In any case, did Ned care for her at all? Where was he, and why had there been no word from him? Perhaps there had been, to her parents. And then into Katherine's mind came the memory of Lord Mewtas's pretty daughter Arabella, with whom Ned had been known to flirt. This way and that, her thoughts sped, as she tossed on her pillows, wakeful. But sleep came to her at last, and she awoke with a smile on her lips, her first thought that Ned Hertford's betrothal to her sister was to be set aside.

Katherine crouched terror-stricken outside her mother's solar. She could hear dreadful things happening to her sister Jane. First, voices raised in shrill altercation, then sobs, now the swish of a birch and low moans. Jane was being beaten for her refusal to marry Guildford Dudley.

It was terrible. Katherine put her hands to her ears to shut out these appalling sounds and crept away. There was nothing she could do. Nothing that anybody could do. Their parents were all-powerful. In the end Jane would have to give in. She might as well have done so in the beginning and saved herself this pain. Next, a husband would be chosen for Katherine, too, and she would be forced to accept him, whosoever he might be. It had been madness to suppose for one instant that she would be able to make her own choice. He would be a nobleman, of course, and rich, or her parents would never consider him. But whosoever it was, it would not be Ned. And whosoever it was, she would be compelled to marry him. Her tears fell, for her sister, and for herself.

At last Jane came, slowly, unsteadily, with faltering gait, and was put to bed, gently, by their old nurse, Mrs Ellen. Jane had no fight left in her, only a great weariness, and indifference. She would obey her parents.

In the weeks that followed, Lady Jane was quiet and withdrawn, but her parents appeared well-satisfied, and were more tolerant than of late to their daughters. To Jane, perhaps to make up for their harsh insistence upon her betrothal to Guildford Dudley, they were especially kind. And Lady Katherine's budding beauty was to them a source of great satisfaction.

They entertained more lavishly than ever. The Earl of Pembroke, one of Northumberland's chief allies, was among their guests, and with him, his son, Lord Herbert.

There was dancing after supper and Lord Herbert partnered Katherine as he had done at Christmas, stepping gracefully in the stately pavane, but tossing her high in the more boisterous galliard. Faster and faster went the fiddlers, and the dancers galloped madly round the hall, finishing out of breath and helpless with laughter. Oh! It was a gay evening and never had Katherine looked lovelier. Her full skirt, a deep blue, matching the blue of her eyes, was cut away in front, revealing a rose-pink under petticoat. Her hair gleamed golden-red and her cheeks were rosy with the glow of youth. To be sure, she and Herbert made a pretty pair, well-matched, thought the Duke and Duchess of Suffolk, looking on benignly. The Earl of Pembroke nodded in agreement. Katherine was in her fourteenth year. Old enough to be wed, and Herbert would be well-satisfied to have her as his wife.

Next morning, Katherine's studies were interrupted by a summons to her mother's solar. There she found the Earl of Pembroke and his son Herbert, with the Duke and Duchess of Suffolk. At her entry all eyes were turned upon her, Lord Herbert regarding her with some affection, his father with approval, while the Duke and Duchess of Suffolk looked upon their second daughter with pride. As always, it was the Duchess who dominated the scene, the Duke a pale shadow beside her, ever willing to fall in with her ambitious schemes.

After greetings were exchanged, without further preamble she began, "Daughter, you are a child no longer. The time has come for you to think of marriage. We have found a husband for you. Lord Herbert is willing to take you as his wife. Tell us, are you willing to be wed to him?"

Although phrased as a question, it was heard by Katherine as a command.

She was to marry Lord Herbert. To resist would be useless she well knew, remembering the punishment Jane had received. But to marry Lord Herbert! Why not? He was a pretty fellow, with delicate features, if a weak chin, and his prowess at the galliard and pavane was undisputed. They had fun together, he was handsome and rich and she would have an assured position as his wife. But to *marry* him! So this was to be the end of her daydreams. Her mind in a turmoil, she was quite unable to give an answer, but stood dumbly.

"Well, answer me, daughter," her mother said impatiently. "Have you no mind to be wed?"

"Yes, I — I have," said Katherine, and it was true. To be married, to have an establishment of her own, to be away from her domineering mother, to be free from the boredom of her studies, all this was to be ardently desired, and if it was not to be Ned, it might as well be the Earl of Pembroke's son.

And now Lord Herbert, taking this hesitant answer for acceptance, took her hand and put it to his lips, then placed a ring upon her finger. Katherine was betrothed.

After much consultation it was arranged that Katherine's and Jane's marriage ceremonies should take place at the same time, in the chapel of the Duke of Northumberland's London mansion, Durham House, in the Strand, on Whit Sunday. There was no time to be lost, for there were many preparations to be made, and it was already past Easter. Besides the weddings of Katherine and Jane, as a make-weight, Mary, the little sister who did not grow, was to be betrothed to her cousin, Lord Arthur Grey, many years her senior. The Suffolks removed from Bradgate to their town house for greater convenience.

Meanwhile the Duke of Northumberland spared no expense in his preparations. Durham House was replenished with tapestries and Turkish carpets; the walls and furniture in the state rooms were covered in gold and crimson tissue, and a new front, sewn with pearls, was hung upon the altar in the Chapel.

Moreover he contrived that rich gifts

should be sent to the brides-to-be, ostensibly from the king, but in fact, from Somerset's confiscated property. They were received by the Duchess of Suffolk rapturously, and she called Jane and Katherine to admire them.

"See, my daughters, what your cousin, the king, has been pleased to send us," she exclaimed, plunging her hands into a wooden chest, and bringing out strings of pearls and sparkling diamonds.

Katherine's eyes shone with delight. She loved pretty things, and for the first time in her life, she was being given the same attention as her elder sister, Jane, and was enjoying a sense of importance. She had thrust from herself all thoughts of Lord Hertford, and if the truth be known, thought very little about her husband-to-be, Lord Herbert Pembroke. She lived for the moment, and this moment was to be savoured to the full.

"Look Jane!" she cried, pulling from the chest a generous length of cloth of gold. There were more rolls of cloth beneath, lengths of cloth of silver and rich velvets.

Jane was less ecstatic. Rich clothes were anathema to her, and she resented deeply her forced engagement to Guildford Dudley, whom she despised heartily as a dolt and a weakling.

"It is kind of the king," was all she had to say of his rich presents, refusing to join in the jubilation. Doubtless her mother and sister would have been less delighted, had they realized that the gifts were booty from the hapless Earl of Somerset's estates, and should have been the property of Ned Hertford's mother.

An army of sewing-women was installed in Suffolk House, and they worked long hours, stitching beautiful robes for the Duchess and her daughters. The brides were to wear dresses of gold and silver brocade, liberally sewn with pearls and diamonds.

Upon Whit-Sunday, the wedding morning, Mrs Ellen was up betimes, supervising the toilet of her young charges, bathing them in water delicately perfumed with sweet-smelling herbs, and insisting that none but she should comb their hair, which she strung with pearls, and left free flowing over their shoulders.

At last they were ready, and attended by their parents and their ladies, took barge to Durham House.

Here, a splendid banquet was laid out. In the kitchens, cooks and scullions were intent upon their tasks — turn-spits were roasting great carcases of venison. Dishes of swan and peacock were prepared; young pigs were soused in wine, and flavoured with bay leaves, ginger, nutmeg and cloves. Leaves for the salats must be freshly gathered from the vegetable garden, and Dickon, a young apprentice cook was entrusted with this task.

Happy to be released from the heat and turmoil of the kitchen, if only for a short while, he skipped outside happily, a wicker trug upon his arm. The air was fragrant with the scent of hawthorn, and golden laburnum drooped, heavy with blossom, by his path.

Dickon was not familiar with all the plants he had been told to pick, but not wishing to reveal his ignorance, he gathered what he took to be the right leaves, including some hemlock water dropwort, an umbelliferous plant which he mistook for alexanders. There was no time to be lost. Already the guests were arriving for the ceremony, and the wedding breakfast must be ready. Dickon filled his basket hurriedly, topping it up with one or two sprays of laburnum which he thought very pretty, and returned to the kitchen.

Meanwhile the state rooms were filling up with lords and ladies, splendid in their silks and velvets, outdoing each other in the brilliance of their jewels. All the rich and noble families in the land were represented here. The Winchesters, the Pembrokes, the Huntingdons; and outshining them all in grandeur and in arrogance, handsome and self-assured, the many members of the Northumberland family. These were the rulers of England, the members of the Privy Council, who told the king what he must do. All were here to celebrate the marriages with feasting and dancing, saving the presence of the young king himself and he could not come because he lay dying in his palace at Greenwich.

First came the handfasting of the little Lady Mary to the tall grave stranger who stood by her side. Then Katherine and Jane, attended by their bridegrooms stood before the altar. And now the priest was intoning the marriage service. "Dearly beloved, we are gathered here in the sight of God, and in the face of this company, to join together — "

As though awakening suddenly from a dream, Katherine realized that she was being married, joined irrevocably, to Herbert Pembroke. It was all wrong. She did not want to be joined forever to Herbert Pembroke. It was Ned Hertford who should be standing by her side, not this weakling, Herbert. She looked about her desperately, like a little wild creature in a trap. She had walked into it with her eyes open, lured by the thought of freedom from her tyrannical mother, and by the status which marriage would give her. Now it was too late to draw back.

Inexorably, the priest continued, "Wilt thou have this woman forsaking all other . . . so long as ye both shall live?"

"Wilt thou have this man — obey him, and serve him, love, honour, and keep him in sickness and in health; and forsaking all other . . . so long as both shall live?"

Why, oh why, had she allowed this to happen? She should have been strong, defying everybody, enduring all, rather than be joined for life to this man she did not love. She must have been asleep, sleep-walking, and now it was too late.

"Those whom God hath joined together, let no man put asunder," intoned the priest. Then it was all over, Lord Herbert's ring on Katherine's finger. The bridecup with its sprigs of rosemary floating in it, was being passed about, the brides were being kissed, and the bridegrooms congratulated.

Now it was time for the wedding feast. The Duke and Duchess of Northumberland led the way, followed by the bridal couples. Behind them walked the Duke and Duchess of Suffolk, well-pleased with themselves, and the weddings they had just witnessed. Like pieces in a game of chess, their daughters had been placed strategically, to further their parents' overweening ambition. No matter to them that Jane looked pale and mournful on this her wedding day, or that Katherine, hardly in her teens, and already beautiful as a rose, had the panic-stricken look of a trapped young animal.

They all sat down to the wedding feast, the Duke and Duchess of Northumberland sharing the top of a great table with the Duke and Duchess of Suffolk, Jane and Dudley on their right, and Herbert and Katherine on their left.

The cloth was glittering with great silver and gilt salts and wine cups engraved with scenes from the hunt, fine embroidered napkins, and knives with handles of carved ivory. Subtleties of hardened sugar graced the table, in the form of animals such as lions, unicorns, antelopes and tigers, and for a first course there were dishes of exotic salats, with buds from violets and other flowers, and green leaves from rosemary, sage, borage and endive, with dressings coloured by saffron and flavoured by musk and rose vinegar. Next followed venison, sucking-pigs, swans and peacocks, and pigeon pies. Then sweets of quince and cherry and custard tarts, and comfits of marchpane and pastry.

Katherine ate mechanically all that was put before her, refusing nothing, tasting nothing, drinking much sack, and conscious only of a deep pit of misery.

Lady Katherine struggled to lift the great stone which she knew she must throw to destroy the dreadful creature who glared, hot-eyed, from the dark corner. Slowly she raised the rock above her head, straining against the pain in her belly, and was about to throw it, when her foot slipped, and she fell, down, down, down, to awaken with a nauseating shock. Where was she and what had happened? She was in a strange room, in a strange bed. Only old Nurse Ellen, moving quietly about the chamber, was familiar. Fact and fancy, nightmare and reality were inextricably mixed. Katherine shut her eyes, then opened them again and looked about her. It was night and candles flickered in their sconces on the walls. Across a chest was flung a dress, richly ornamented, the jewels in its embroidery winking and flashing in the candlelight. Of course. It was her wedding dress. She remembered it all now. She had worn it for her marriage to Lord Herbert. They had stood in a row before the altar in the chapel of the Duke of Northumberland's town house; herself with Herbert Pembroke; Jane, white-faced, by the side of handsome Guildford Dudley, and Mary, the little sister who did not grow, too young to be married, was betrothed to her cousin, Lord Arthur Grey. After the weddings, they had all sat down to a sumptuous repast, and then — and then — what had happened next and where was she?

"Nellie!" she called weakly to the old nurse. "Nellie!"

"My lady, my little lady, the Lord be praised. Awake at last!" cried Mrs Ellen, hurrying to the bedside.

"What happened? Where am I?" whispered Katherine.

"Hush. Do not try to talk. Lie quietly." The old woman leaned over her and put a cool compress to her head, which was burning.

"What happened? Where am I?" Katherine repeated.

"You've been ill, my dearie, so ill," Nurse Ellen said, "because a scullion picked a wrong leaf for the salat for the wedding feast."

"A wrong leaf?"

"He was sent to gather sage and thyme, parsley, mint and bay leaf from the herb garden, but by mistake he plucked some bitter weed which made you all ill, brides and bridesgrooms, and many of the wedding guests, too."

Katherine laughed weakly. "But where am I?"

"You were put into a litter and brought to your father-in-law's house. You are at Baynard's Castle, near the Temple Gardens."

"And my — my husband? What of him?" ventured Katherine.

"In bed ill, too."

"But not in my bed. Not yet. At least that is something to be thankful for," said the Lady Katherine.

"Hush, you must not say such things. When you feel better, you'll be pleased enough to have a handsome young husband such as he."

"Is he very ill? More ill than me? Oh, if he would but die!"

"For shame, child," rebuked Mrs Ellen

sharply, reverting to her nursery authority, forgetful that her charge was now a married woman.

"Oh, Nellie, I'm so unhappy," and the Lady Katherine, bride of Lord Herbert, pulled the coverlets over her face and began to sob.

"There, there, my dearie, don't take on so. You'll make yourself ill again."

"I wish that I had died. I do, I do."

"There try to go to sleep again. You'll feel better in the morning."

"Where is my sister Jane? And my parents and Mary?"

"The Lady Jane is with her husband in her father-in-law's house, and the Duke and Duchess of Suffolk have taken the Lady Mary back to the nursery in their house at Sheen."

Exhausted by her illness and by her tears, Lady Katherine was soon in a deep sleep, from which she did not awaken until the next day was well advanced. She felt better, though weak, and did not leave her bed that day.

Next morning, Katherine was awakened by bright sunlight streaming into her chamber. She felt well, clearheaded and hungry and was ready for the bowl of frumenty which Nurse Ellen presently brought for her. The old nurse was pleased when she was presented with an empty dish.

"There, my lamb, you'll soon be feeling strong again, now you've got something inside you," she said cheerfully.

"I feel strong now, Nellie," was the reply, "and I want to get up."

"So you shall. So you shall, my little lady," and Nurse Ellen bustled away to fetch clean linen and a suitable gown.

Katherine stretched out her left hand and spread her fingers. She regarded her wedding ring of solid gold. It looked too heavy for the slim and delicate finger which it encircled.

"So I am a married woman," she said aloud. It was no dream, no nightmare, but a solemn fact. Her childhood was over, and she had entered a new life.

Her musing was interrupted by Mrs Ellen, returning with a fine gown of cream velvet, which she spread upon the bed for her charge's approval.

"And my — my husband?" ventured Katherine, robed now, and looking very pretty, if a little frail, after her illness. "How is he? Know you if he is recovered, too?"

"Yes, my lady, he is recovered, and asking after your health. Do you feel well enough to meet with him?"

Katherine had a sharp sense of apprehension, mixed with curiosity. Sometime she must meet with her husband. It may as well be now, she thought.

"Bring him to me," she commanded, and seated herself regally in a large chair, with a wooden foot-rest. Almost a throne, she thought, arranging her skirts carefully. She waited with some impatience for what seemed a very long time.

At last he came, entering the apartment hesitantly. Katherine held out a hand to him, and he bowed over it, then raised it to his lips.

"I trust you are well recovered?" he asked.

"Yes, I thank you. Are you well now?"

"Well enough," he replied, then added, a little awkwardly, with an attempt at gallantry, "better since I beheld the beauty of my beloved wife."

Katherine blushed, and was at a loss for an answer, so a silence fell between them. The light camaraderie they had felt for each other when dancing to the gay music of the galliard had quite disappeared in this new situation of man and wife. The constraint was broken simultaneously by both of them.

"Will you — " began Katherine. "May I — " said Herbert.

They both laughed nervously. "May I escort you to the garden?" asked Herbert.

"Yes, please do. That is what I was about to ask you," replied Katherine, rising from her chair, and placing a hand upon his arm.

He guided her through a large but rather gloomy hall, out upon a terrace, then down some steps to a knot garden of intricate design, meticulously executed.

"It — it is very pretty," said Katherine, and could find nothing more to say.

Herbert, too, was tongue-tied with shyness. But they could not remain here for the rest of the day, staring without words at the knot garden, admirable as it might be.

"Do you bowl?" he asked at last.

“Oh, yes,” replied Katherine, “though I have not much skill at thc game.”

So Herbert guided her to the green and they played a desultory game of bowls. But Katherine soon tired, for her illness had left her weak, so she excused herself and returned to her apartments, to be fussed over by Mrs Ellen, who insisted upon her retiring to her bed at a very early hour, lest she had overtired herself.

Before leaving her young mistress, Mrs Ellen ventured to say, “Your husband is a very handsome young gentleman, madam.”

“Yes,” answered Katherine, and shut her eyes.

The old nurse sighed and left her.

Katherine lay wakeful, tense and uneasy, her ears strained, waiting. She was a married woman now. Was her bed about to be invaded by her husband, this stranger, who, it seemed had as little to say to her, as she to him?

At last she fell asleep, and awoke next morning, alone in her bed. And so the days passed, her husband making perfunctory appearances, always polite, if awkward and shy, disappearing on his own business for long periods, and making no attempt to consummate their marriage.

Katherine had little to do, to amuse and occupy herself. Upon her marriage she had been provided with two young serving women, to attend her and look after her clothes, and these, with Mrs Ellen, were her sole companions, for the Earl of Pembroke was a widower and had little company in his house. At first she was relieved to find so little was expected of her, but soon became bored and piqued by her husband's apparent lack of interest in her. This situation went on, day after day, until at last Lady Katherine was provoked to say to her husband, "We are lawfully wed. Why do you not wish to come to my bed?"

The young man blushed to the roots of his golden hair, and said, hesitantly, "Forgive me. It is not lack of desire for you, but my father — he has forbidden me. He says we must wait a little. You are very young — "

"I am nearly fifteen. But I am very content as I am. Perhaps when your father decides that the time has come you will not find me willing."

"I am sorry. I have vexed you. Believe me — "

"Not at all. We will stay as we are so long as your *father* pleases. I, too, was forced to obey the will of my parents, or I would not be here at all."

3

THE Duke of Pembroke was summoned to Greenwich, leaving Katherine and her husband at Baynard's Castle. Katherine was surprised and delighted to receive a roll of green and gold brocade with instructions to have a new robe made from it instantly. She summoned her women and soon they were stitching busily, and in every great house in London sewing women bent to their tasks of making new gowns for their ladies. It was whispered that the young king was lying dead at Greenwich, and for the first time, a queen was about to be proclaimed sovereign of England.

"Poor Edward," sighed Katherine, as she pivoted slowly round in her new dress. "The Lady Mary will be queen, I suppose."

"Perhaps," said Mrs Ellen, and stood back critically, to make sure the hem was straight.

"What do you mean 'perhaps'?"

"Strange stories are going round, Madam, that your sister, Lady Janc, has been left the throne by King Edward's will."

"Jane?"

"So it is said."

"But what of Lady Mary and Lady Elizabeth?" questioned Katherine. "Princess Mary is next in succession to the throne. She is Edward's elder sister, and after her comes Princess Elizabeth."

"Half-sisters, and one of them a bastard," said Mrs Ellen cryptically. "Will you step out of the gown now, Madam, carefully?"

How Mrs Ellen came to be possessed of this secret information Katherine never discovered, but it proved to be correct, for at last the news was out. The king was dead, and Lady Jane, wife of Lord Guildford Dudley, was to be proclaimed Queen of England.

Looking extremely pretty in her new gown, Katherine waited with Lord Herbert, in a group of lords and ladies, to welcome her sister at the Tower of London. Queen Jane arrived in the brilliant sunshine of a July afternoon by a state barge, gilded and aflutter with brightly coloured standards and streamers. At her side sat her husband, Guildford Dudley, elegant in doublet and hose of shining white. More painted and gilded barges followed, crowded with lords and ladies, in velvets and silks and brocades, jewels flashing and sparkling, a feast of beauty for the people who lined the banks of the river, staring silently.

As the cavalcade landed it was greeted by a deafening discharge of artillery from the Tower batteries, but a shadow was cast momentarily over the brilliant scene, as frightened ravens rose croaking and flapping their great black wings.

"How lovely she looks," whispered Katherine, then bent her knee in a deep curtsey, as her sister walked past, into the Tower, with stately gait, her head held high. Her husband walked by her side, bowing to the ground whenever she noticed him, her mother behind, bearing her train of cloth of gold, heavily ornamented with precious gems.

"Mother carrying Jane's train!" Katherine was incredulous. A picture flashed into her mind of her sister creeping into bed, bruised and defeated after the whipping by her parents. This was indeed a new Jane, a different person from the studious, quiet girl, who preferred her books to any other pursuit.

"She is wonderful," her sister acknowledged, "but how did she get so tall?"

"They have strapped chopines, wooden clogs, beneath her shoes," said Lord Herbert, "which must have raised her a good three inches. I caught sight of them as she was handed from the barge. Come, let us follow into the Tower."

Inside, in the state apartments, the nobility of London thronged about their new queen, and here, unexpectedly, Lady Katherine caught a glimpse of Lord Hertford. She had not set eyes upon him since that day, it seemed a life time ago, when she had said goodbye to him, and he had ridden post-haste to London, to his father's defence. But here he was, to do homage to her sister, Queen Jane. So his father's disgrace must have been forgotten, since here he was at court. A great thrill ran through Katherine, and impulsively she left her husband's side and started towards Hertford. She stopped abruptly when she realized that Ned was escorting Lord Mewtas's pretty daughter, the Lady Arabella, and both seemed as merry as crickets. Katherine stared at them miserably, her heart was black jealousy. Ned Hertford must have felt the intensity of her gaze, for he turned and their eyes met across the crowded room. Making an excuse to his companion, he made a move towards Katherine.

"Ned," she said. "Oh, Ned!" and suddenly tears welled up in her eyes.

"What is it, Kate?" he asked. "Don't cry. You mustn't cry." But tears were pouring down Katherine's cheeks.

Ned Hertford looked at her in astonishment and consternation, then hastily shepherded her towards a little anteroom leading off the great hall.

"There, there, sweetheart," he said gently, "what has upset you so?"

"Oh, Ned, I'm so unhappy," gulped Katherine. "They made me marry — I didn't want to marry Herbert Pembroke — "

"Oh, come now, Kate. It's not so bad

as all that, surely. Here you are, the second lady in the land and — ”

“What mean you — the second lady?”

“You are next in succession to the throne, of course, after your sister Jane. You are a lady of great moment now, and here you are, weeping.”

“Why, yes, I suppose I am,” said Katherine, in some wonderment, “but it matters not to me. Oh Ned, I do love you so. Why couldn’t you have married me?”

“Hush, Kate. What are you saying? You are a married woman now. Not my little playmate any longer.”

“Your little playmate? Is that all I was to you. That night — have you forgotten? Did it mean nothing to you? Nothing at all?”

“Of course I haven’t forgotten and it meant a great deal to me. Why, you saved my life that night, did you not, Kate? And I was — I am, very fond of you. You surely know that.”

“Fond of me? Fond of me? Oh, Ned! And are you fond of my sister Jane? And you are fond of the Lady Arabella Mewtas, too, I suppose. Oh, I could hate you, if I did not love you so much. But what does it matter now? As you say, I am a married woman. Let us talk of other things. Is not my sister truly regal? Every inch a queen?"

"Yes, she is in truth a very queen. But she is not so pretty as you are, my sweet, my little rose bud."

He put a finger beneath her chin and turned her face up towards him, then gently, oh, so gently, kissed her on her lips, and would have put her from him. But Katherine flung her arms about his neck, and clung to him, and suddenly they were locked in a passionate embrace, oblivious to all about them. They were brought back to earth by Lord Pembroke's voice, trembling with fury.

"So, madam, this is how you behave behind your husband's back, is it?"

Ned and Katherine sprang apart.

"Get out! Get out of here and back to your husband slut. As for you, sir, you — you — pah! Get out of my sight, and never let me see you with my daughter-in-law again."

The enraged earl strode from the room snorting and muttering, shushing Lady

Katherine in front of him, back to her husband.

Outside the Tower, a hostile crowd listened while with fanfare of trumpets, heralds proclaimed:

"Jane, by the Grace of God, Queen of England, France and Ireland, Defender of the Faith, and of the Church of England and also of Ireland, under Christ, on earth the supreme head."

Other heralds were sent throughout the country to proclaim Lady Jane as rightful Queen of the realm. But there were no hurrahs for her, this almost unknown young woman who had usurped the place of old King Harry's daughter Mary.

So the first day of Queen Jane's reign ended. Lady Katherine and Lord Herbert remained in the Tower to support her, together with the Duke and Duchess of Suffolk, the Duke and Duchess of Northumberland, the Duke of Pembroke, and all the rest of the Privy Council.

They were unaware that in the darkness of the night, Princess Mary, disappointed elder sister of the deceased king, slipped away from London in disguise, riding hastily through Cambridge and Bury

St Edmunds towards her castle at Framlingham in Suffolk.

Lady Katherine could not sleep. She tossed and turned upon her bed, tortured by the memory of Lord Hertford's dark eyes and the feel of his arms around her. She was apprehensive, too. How angry Lord Pembroke had been when he had found them in each other's arms.

At last she slept, heavily, and dreamt that she was imprisoned in a dark dungeon in the depths of the Tower inhabited by rats, who glared at her with bright evil eyes, from each corner of the cell. She shrieked, and awakened, to be comforted by Nurse Ellen, ever watchful, on a truckle bed by the side of the fourposter upon which Katherine lay.

"I'm frightened, Nelly," she cried, and clung to her old nurse. "I dreamt I was a prisoner in a dreadful dungeon."

"Don't take on so, mistress, there's nothing to fear. Remember, your sister is Queen of England, now, and you are the next in succession. You must deport yourself like a queen. No more of this, madam. There, go to sleep again. Old Nelly will look after you."

But Katherine could sleep no more. Jane, Queen of England! It was all wrong, of course. The crown should have gone to her cousin, Mary. How had Northumberland prevailed upon the Privy Council to kneel to her sister Jane? It was the wish of the young deceased king, he had said. Edward had put in his will that Jane should succeed him. But had he the right to exclude his half-sisters, Mary and Elizabeth? What did they think about it, and what were the people of England thinking about it? Had they no voice at all in the succession of their rulers? Did they even care? Or were they content to cheer and wave, whoever might be set before them? But there had been no cheering and waving by the crowds who had lined the river bank yesterday, to welcome their new queen, Jane. They were silent, Katherine remembered, standing and staring without voice or movement.

Katherine sighed. It was all wrong, just as it had been wrong for her to be forced to marry Lord Herbert, and for Jane to marry Guildford Dudley. Katherine's thoughts turned to her personal unhappiness. Was Ned angry with her for putting him into so humiliating a position? It had been all her fault. Had he gone back to that minx, Lady Arabella? Would Ned marry *her*? It was a relief when morning came and Katherine could get up and put these thoughts away from her.

As Mrs Ellen combed her red-gold hair, Katherine asked, "What news, Nelly? What is it like out there beyond the Tower walls?"

Nurse Ellen sighed. "They say the streets were crowded last night, madam. Everyone was out, but there was no rejoicing, no bonfires lit at the street corners, for lads and lassies to dance around. Instead they thronged the pillory at Cheapside and tried to release a boy called Gilbert Potter, an ale-drawer, who stood there, pinned by the ears. But he was guarded by soldiers who kept the crowds away."

"What had he done?"

"When the proclamation was read yesterday at Cheapside, everybody was quiet. Nobody cheered when they were called Queen Jane's loving, faithful and obedient subjects. But when the Lady Mary's claim was called untrue because she was a bastard, angry muttering began, and this Gilbert Potter shouted out 'the Lady Mary has the better title'. Then the crowd all shouted 'aye, aye!' but soldiers rode among them and dragged the poor lad away to the pillory."

"Is he there still?"

"Nay, he was released last night, but 'tis said his ears were cut off before they let him go."

"Poor lad. And he is right, Nelly. The Lady Mary has the better title. But my poor sister Jane was bullied into it."

"Aye," agreed the old servant, heavily.

Queen Jane, too, had spent a restless, troubled night after the first day of her reign. She awoke with a splitting headache, and when Winchester, the Lord High Treasurer, brought her the jewels and the crown she received him and them without enthusiasm.

"Why bring me the crown?" she asked. "I have not demanded it."

"To see how it fits Your Grace."

Jane was reluctant to put the crown upon her head, but at last was persuaded to do so, and sat erect upon her chair, wearing the emblem of sovereignty.

"I will have another made forthwith," said the Lord High Treasurer, "to crown your husband with."

Jane was now wearing the crown Imperial of the Realm and she immediately assumed the dignity and authority of her position. Very well, she would be a queen. She was a puppet no longer.

Queen Jane announced quietly but with great firmness, "One crown is all that will be required."

"But your husband — ?" stammered Winchester.

"Shall be a duke," answered the queen.

The Lord High Treasurer retired in some confusion, and Guildford Dudley, who was present, turned upon his young wife in a great fury.

"You shall make me king," he spluttered.

"Only Parliament," she said firmly, "can give you that position."

"I will be made king by you and by Act of Parliament," he persisted.

"And through you, your father would rule this country," returned Jane, harshly. "If you are to be king, it will be by Act of

Parliament and not by me."

Queen Jane began to weep bitterly. The plot was revealed to her in all its duplicity. She had been given to Northumberland's favourite son, and she had been made queen, solely to further the Duke of Northumberland's grandiose ambitions. Through them he would be virtually the ruler of England. No consideration of her or her happiness had crossed his mind. She thought of the pretty speeches her husband had lately made to her and wondered if his father had composed them for him.

Guildford Dudley, beside himself with disappointment and irritation with his wife's obstinacy, burst into tears himself and rushed from the room to find his mother.

Queen Jane dried her eyes and sent for her Privy Councillors, Lord Arundel and her sister's father-in-law, Lord Pembroke.

"If the Crown belongs to me," she said, "I would be content to make my husband a duke. But I will never consent to make him king."

Pembroke was dismayed by this refusal, but Arundel, a reluctant accomplice of

Northumberland's, was secretly amused. Guildford Dudley returned, accompanied by his mother. They entreated, reproached and abused her, but they could not shake her resolve to do nothing unconstitutional. She would not have Guildford crowned king without the consent of Parliament.

"I will make you a duke," Queen Jane repeated, "the Duke of Clarence, if you desire it."

"I will not be a duke, I will be king," he replied petulantly.

"No," said the Queen.

The Duchess of Northumberland lost patience. "Come," she said, "we will return to Sion House. If you are not to be king, you shall no longer sleep with her."

She swept out of the room with her son. Queen Jane turned to her privy councillors and commanded them to bring back her husband. They obeyed her command, and Guildford Dudley and the Duchess of Northumberland returned and accepted her decision.

Queen Jane felt no joy in her triumph.

4

QUEEN JANE was apprehensive and far from well. She confided to her sister Katherine that her hair was coming out by the handful, and her skin was peeling.

"What is the cause of it? What ails you?" asked Katherine in consternation.

Jane hesitated and sighed heavily.

"What is it?" repeated Katherine.

Then Jane said, "I fear I am being poisoned."

"Poisoned! But why? And by whom?"

"By my father-in-law," Jane whispered, "such is his wrath at my refusal to make my husband king."

In fact the Duke of Northumberland had other matters which demanded his full attention. It was evident that all was far from well outside the Tower walls. The people of London and the provinces refused to accept their new queen. Heralds were sent out again to proclaim Jane as 'rightful Queen of this realm'.

Insurrections broke out in several places and proclamations were made in various towns that the Lady Mary was the rightful heir. She had raised her standard at her castle in Framlingham, in Suffolk, and all the chivalry of Norfolk and Suffolk were mustering round her. In Norwich she was proclaimed Queen of England.

The country must be raised against the Princess Mary without a moment's delay. Preparations were hastily made for an advance into East Anglia, to be led by the Duke of Suffolk. The Lords waited on Queen Jane to acquaint her with their decision and obtain her official approval. Jane was so dismayed by the thought of being left in Northumberland's power that she burst into tears and refused to give her sanction.

"My father must tarry at home in my company," she said, "while my lord, the Duke of Northumberland takes the field."

Nothing would change the queen's determination to keep her father by her side. The Duke of Northumberland was reluctant to depart from London, fearing the disloyalty of his fellow conspirators if he turned his back on them, but he was forced to acccpt the queen's decision. Regally clad in a scarlet cloak he left the city, leading three thousand soldiers, two thousand horses and a great train of artillery. A great silent conflux of people watched him go. Nobody raised a hand in farewell, or wished him godspeed.

The Council was loyal to Jane, but its members were uneasy, especially when Northumberland wrote complaining of fearful desertions, describing the Princess Mary's daily increasing strength and entreating the Council to send him reinforcements.

They persuaded Ridley, Bishop of London, to preach a sermon at Paul's Cross, extolling the foresight of their late king in leaving the crown to a Protestant queen, and outlining the evils that must have occurred from the succession of the Princess Mary, with her zeal for the Papacy, and her foreign connections. He spoke with eloquent enthusiasm of the virtues, talents, and piety of the young Queen Jane, and the blessings to be anticipated from her righteous sway. But the people heard him coldly, and there were no shouts of 'God save Queen Jane'.

Indeed, the sermon only served to heighten the feelings of the citizens of London against her, and they began to demonstrate in the streets. Soldiers were sent out to quell the riots and blood flowed freely. Bonfires were lit, and crowds of young men and woman, glad of any excuse for horseplay, whirled round the flames shouting "Queen Mary! Queen Mary!"

Queen Jane and her sister, Lady Katherine, with their ladies, sat in the state apartments in the Tower and listened to the tumult.

"What are they shouting?" asked Katherine.

The answer floated to them through the windows in a long thin scream of "Queen Mary, Queen Mary!"

"They hate me. How they hate me," cried the young queen bitterly, clapping her hands over her ears. "I never wanted to be their queen. I have never harmed them. I was coerced and bullied and persuaded by my father-in-law. Oh, that I had never listened to him or to my parents."

A fresh outburst of screaming broke out. The Queen's ladies began to cry, huddling together and wailing, "What shall we do? Who will save us?"

Queen Jane took command of the situation. "Lock the doors," she cried. "Lock all the doors, and bring the keys to me. Quickly! And send my Lords Pembroke and Winchester to me at once."

Up and down stairs, along passages, into apartments, scurried frightened servants, spreading their panic, until the whole Tower was in an uproar, but my Lords Pembroke and Winchester were not to be found. Without telling one another, they had each left separately for his own house. Queen Jane had a sudden terrified realization that she, the innocent tool of these ruthless, ambitious men, was going to be abandoned now that the tide was running against them.

Messengers were sent from the Tower to Pembroke's and Winchester's mansions, and they brought back not only those noble lords, but the news that a placard had been found stuck on Queenhithe Church, importing that Mary had been proclaimed Queen of England and Ireland in every town and city therein excepting London.

The clamour gradually subsided and Queen Jane and Lady Katherine and their ladies retired to bed. Not so the Privy Council, who met by stealth to plan their next move. In the morning they waited on the queen in a body to explain to her that it was necessary for them to leave the Tower to beg help immediately from Monsieur de Noailles, the French Ambassador. Resigned, Queen Jane agreed to their departure.

"You and your wife will return to Baynard's Castle immediately," Lord Pembroke commanded his son.

"I must stay with my sister," declared Katherine defiantly.

"You will do as you are bid, madam," her father-in-law said curtly.

"Go with them," said Queen Jane, "there is no help for it."

"Then I shall leave Nelly behind. She will take care of you."

Mrs Ellen had been nurse to each of the sisters in turn, had mothered them and scolded them and told stories to them on long winter's evenings. Queen Jane was glad of her comforting presence.

The Privy Council assembled at Baynard's Castle where it was decided after some deliberation that John Dudley, Duke of Northumberland, was a traitor to Queen Mary. He had led them all astray and betrayed their honour. They then set off to St Paul's Cathedral where they ordered Mass to be celebrated, and publicly thanked God that their eyes had been opened to the evil of their ways.

The Duke of Northumberland, now in Cambridge, his army fast melting away, sensing the Council's defection in London, personally proclaimed Queen Mary in the market-place, tossing up his cap, while tears ran down his cheeks. But Lord Arundel, riding post-haste to Cambridge, arrested him and brought him back to London ignominously, where he was imprisoned in the Tower.

The Lady Mary was proclaimed queen in London and the provinces and the Privy Council sent her their loyal submission. The reign of Queen Jane was over.

The Duke of Suffolk entered his

daughter's apartments where he found her at supper seated beneath her canopy of state. With his own hands he tore it down and said "The Lady Mary has been proclaimed. You are no longer queen. You must put off your royal robes and be content with a private life."

For a few seconds there was silence between them. Jane looked at her father steadily while she weighed his words 'be content with a private life'. There was nothing which would content her more. Then this hideous nightmare was really over? Her feelings were a mixture of relief and resentment. At last she spoke. "Sir, I welcome this message more than my advancement to royalty. Out of obedience to you and my mother, I have grievously sinned and acted against my own desires. Now I most willingly relinquish the crown and will do my utmost to remedy the mistakes *made by others*, if such faults can be resolved by a willing and open acknowledgment of them." She paused, then asked, "May I go home now?"

Her father looked away from her and muttered, "It would be better to remain here for the present."

Jane retired to her private apartments, where her ladies were awaiting her.

"I am no longer Queen of England," she said. There was a chorus of dismay.

"Do not grieve on my account," she comforted them cheerfully, "for I am very happy to be deposed."

The Duke of Suffolk, having acquainted his daughter with the position, went outside the Tower gates, followed by his soldiers, all unarmed, to affirm his loyalty to the queen.

"I am but one man," he said, "but I here proclaim the Lady Mary's Grace, Queen of England."

He then made off to Sheen, followed by his wife, the Duchess of Suffolk, leaving their daughter Jane in the Tower.

Thomas Bridges, the deputy-lieutenant of the Tower was embarrassed. He had received instructions to imprison the Lady Jane in his lodgings, and he did not know how best to inform her of this necessity. But Jane was not unduly alarmed, trusting in the clemency of her cousin, the queen.

"And my ladies?" asked Jane. "Are they to accompany me?"

"No more than four," was the answer.

"Nurse Ellen — Mrs Tilney, Lady Throgmorton — will you share my captivity?" asked Jane.

They all agreed most willingly.

It was necessary to prepare the state apartments for Queen Mary at once, as news had been received that she had already left Framlingham Castle, and was on her way to London.

Lady Jane's possessions were bundled together without ceremony, among them a casket of Crown Jewels, and she and her ladies were taken at once to their new quarters. In the haste of her departure three other coffers were left behind. They were found by a servant who came to lay fresh rushes. He opened them curiously, for none was locked. In the first box were thirteen pairs of old gloves, some of them odd, and two shaving-cloths, evidently the property at some time, of King Henry VIII. In the second box, a square coffer covered with fustian of Naples, were some keepsakes of one of his queens. There was a love token

— half of a golden ring; some prayer books, and some silver coins; a golden box containing a pair of scissors and some scraps of satin, and a screw of paper holding a pattern of gold damask; a pair of knives in a case of black silk, and other forgotten trifles.

The third coffer was lettered 'Queen's Jewels' and contained chains of gold studded with rosettes of pearl, and other valuables which made the servant's eyes glitter. He hastily spread the abandoned state canopy upon the floor and poured on to it the contents of each coffer, made it into a bundle and carried it away hidden beneath some rushes.

Lady Katherine, alone with her ladies at her father-in-law's gloomy residence, Baynard's Castle, without the comforting presence of Mrs Ellen, was apprehensive and depressed. She had not seen her husband since their somewhat ignominious departure from the Tower. Lord Pembroke had just returned from Essex, from the seat of Sir William Petre, at Ingatestone, where he had ridden post-haste to intercept Queen

Mary on her journey into London. Here the Council, most of whom had lately defied and denied her, were assembled for the purpose of kissing her hand.

Now the Lady Katherine looked sadly from the window of her solar to the street below which was being cleaned and spread with gravel, ready to receive the Lady Mary on her royal progress through the city. A small crowd had gathered outside the house, for it had been rumoured that largesse was to be freely bestowed. Lady Katherine saw her father-in-law come out of the mansion, bareheaded. His cap was in his hand and it was full of angels. He scattered them among the delighted crowd, who ran hither and thither, shoving and scrambling to gather them.

Then, "God save Queen Mary!" cried the Earl, and "God save Queen Mary!" echoed the people.

"Poor Jane," thought Katherine, "what will become of her?"

She remained at the window watching the animated scene below, until she became suddenly aware that her father-in-law had entered the room.

"You must prepare for a journey," he said without preamble. "You are to leave here at once."

"Leave here? Where am I to go?"

"That is no longer my concern. Your marriage to my son shall be annulled at once. Perhaps my Lord Hertford will find you a bed."

"What, my lord?"

"Your women must get your things together immediately. I want you off my premises before her Grace the Queen arrives in London."

"But why?"

"There is no time to discuss or argue about this matter. Your marriage to my son was a mistake which fortunately can be wiped out and forgotten. Prepare for your journey without delay."

Any delight Katherine might have felt over the prospect of leaving the Earl of Pembroke's gloomy residence and weakling of a son was overlaid by indignation and deep humiliation at the manner of her departure.

"Where is Herbert?" demanded Katherine. "Is it with my husband's consent that I am to be dismissed thus?"

Lord Pembroke glared then strode from the room without vouchsafing any reply, and Katherine realized that her husband's desires or happiness weighed no more with his father than her own. Lord Pembroke's only concern was to deny any connection with the unfortunate Lady Jane and her family.

There was nothing for it but to return ignominiously to Sheen. Katherine summoned her women and told them to prepare at once for a journey. Little more than an hour later she and her attendants and all her things were bundled into a barge and sent up the river to her father's house. Of her husband there was no sign.

At Sheen she found her parents and her little sister Mary, but when she enquired after Jane was told that she was being held in the Tower of London temporarily.

"You mean she is a prisoner?" demanded Katherine.

"She has left the state apartments and is lodged in the house of the Gentleman Gaoler for the time being," explained her father.

"Poor Jane!"

"Shc is perfectly comfortable and content. She has her books, and her women to look after her, Mrs Ellen amongst them, and she is at liberty to take the air on Tower Green."

"When will she be able to come home?"

"No doubt her cousin the queen's first act of mercy will be to set Jane free since she has done no wrong."

London was *en fête* to welcome Queen Mary. As if in extenuation of its brief disloyalty to King Harry's eldest daughter, the city had excelled itself in the exuberance of its preparations, the magnificence of its decorations, with triumphal arches and monumental giants and angels.

At last she came, a little middle-aged lady with a high complexion, dressed in violet velvet. She rode a small white ambling nag, the housings of which were fringed with gold, and at her side rode her sister Elizabeth in all the freshness of her youth. Around them rode a cavalcade of ladies and gentlemen, richly arrayed.

Entering the town triumphantly through the portal of Aldgate, which was hung with streamers from top to bottom, they were greeted with music and a thousand voices shouting their hurrahs. Passing through streets lined with all the crafts of London, in their appropriate liveries, holding banners and streamers, the royal procession reached the Tower of London, where it took possession of the state apartments, still warm from Queen Jane's brief sojourn in them.

But Lady Jane, comfortably housed in the home of the deputy lieutenant Thomas Bridges, and relieved of the unwelcome company of her parents-in-law and her husband, knew peace of mind for the first time since the hour of her accession.

It was soon disturbed by a visit from the Lord Treasurer, Winchester, who made a peremptory demand for the return of the crown jewels, and everything which Jane had received from the royal wardrobe. Since the contents of three coffers were found to be missing, they were made good by the forfeiture of all the money in her possession.

Guildford Dudley, now in the Beauchamp Tower, together with his father and his four brothers, was likewise relieved of all his money, on the pretext that he was responsible for the Crown property not restored by his wife. They were now entirely penniless and at the mercy of their jailers. But Jane was still content, for she was allowed writing materials and a few books, including a prayer book, her Greek Testament, and the Phaedo of Plato.

In the meantime, the Duke and Duchess of Suffolk, restored to favour by Queen Mary, returned to their estate at Bradgate with Katherine and Mary, to await the release of their eldest daughter, Jane.

Katherine was restless and bored. She was no longer a child and could not content herself with the diversions of her life before her marriage to Lord Herbert. Nevertheless, she was still a maid, and one who had been flung aside contemptuously when her sister's fortunes had gone awry, and it seemed nobody else would be likely to come forward to claim her hand in marriage. With the advent of

Catholic Queen Mary, Katherine was too close to Protestant Jane to be looked upon with favour by the nobility of England, now closely gathered round their new queen.

So Katherine was left to languish at Bradgate. She amused herself with her pets, her dogs and her monkey, and roamed the park on horseback. Often her thoughts returned to the day she had been a bridesmaid to Mistress Saintlow, and had saved Ned Hertford from the wolf. That was a night to remember. How happy she had been, how carefree.

5

LADY JANE and her husband, Guildford Dudley, left the Tower which they had entered so triumphantly, by barge as they had come, but in somewhat different circumstances, for they were going to their trial at the Guildhall.

As Lady Jane left the barge to head the little procession, she looked pitifully small without her chopines. Gone was her gorgeous apparel and flashing jewels. She was dressed in black, a black satin hood covered her head, and a little prayer book hung at her girdle. She carried another, reading from it serenely, as she walked along. She was followed by Nurse Ellen and Mrs Tilney. Guards separated them from Guildford Dudley, who followed behind.

Some four hundred halberdiers lined the street, to keep the peace, but the crowds were silent; silent with pity this time, no resentment, but only sympathy with these young people who had been catspaws of their ambitious parents.

The prisoners pleaded guilty and were arraigned and condemned. Lady Jane was sentenced to be burnt on Tower Hill or beheaded, at the queen's pleasure. She was followed back to the water's edge by crowds who were weeping and bewailing her fate. It was, nevertheless, understood by her and by all about the court that the queen meant to pardon her, and she was given every indulgence compatible with safe keeping.

Her father-in-law, the Duke of Northumberland, was not so privileged. After being found guilty of high treason and condemned to the block, he made the most humble solicitations for his life, and in a last abject attempt to preserve it, embraced the religion of the Church of Rome. Lady Jane stood at her window in the Gentleman Gaoler's house and watched her father-in-law, missal in hand, head meekly bowed, on his way to Mass in St Peter-ad-Vincula. She was incredulous and scornful of his apostasy. "I pray God," she said, "I, nor no friend of mine, die so." His change of heart availed him nothing. He was executed next day.

So lenient were the terms of Jane's imprisonment that she was allowed out to take the air during those sultry, late summer days; and as she strolled on Tower Green, this uncrowned queen of nine days' reign, she heard the clamour of the preparations being made for the first coronation of a female sovereign that England had ever known.

Her attendants were allowed to leave the Tower at will, and they reported with some excitement, if little tact, upon the pomp and pageantry of the queen's procession through the city, which took place the day before her coronation.

"In Gracechurch Street, madam, there was a great green angel, perched upon an arch. It had a trumpet and played a tune," began Lady Throgmorton, only to be interrupted by Mrs Tilney, who said, "There were four giants in Fenchurch Street, and the conduits at Cornhill and Cheapside were running with wine, that all could drink."

"I never saw such a sight as her procession," continued Lady Throgmorton, "hundreds and hundreds of gentlemen on horseback came first, and then Queen Mary in a splendid litter, supported between six white horses, all covered with housings of cloth of silver and — "

"My lady is tired and has heard enough," said Nurse Ellen, in a voice of authority.

"No, Nelly, I would hear it all," cried Lady Jane. "And how was the Lady M — no, how was Queen Mary attired? Did she look well?"

"She wore a gown of blue velvet, madam, ermine-trimmed, and on her head a caul of gold network, all beset with pearls and precious stones. And after her the Lady Elizabeth and the Lady — some other ladies in robes of crimson velvet, their horses trapped the same, and many more equestrian damsels and some in chariots, all in kirtles of gold or silver cloth. I never saw such a sight."

What Lady Throgmorton forbore to say was that Jane's sister, the Lady Katherine, rode in the procession, as princess of the blood, immediately behind the Princess Elizabeth, who followed the Queen.

"And at St Paul's Peter the Dutchman waited high up on the weathercock," said Mrs Tilney, "it was dusk by the time the procession got to him, great crowds following all the way, and we saw his gymnastics by flickering torchlight. Fearful it was, to see him right up there, and at the end he came flying down on a rope, and all the crowd shouted their hurrahs at such a remarkable feat."

Lady Jane's expected release from captivity was delayed, for the Queen had other matters on her mind. She was determined to marry Prince Philip of Spain, a project which filled her subjects with alarm. The joy felt at her accession waned, and her popularity quickly diminished. Priests were stoned in protest, and a dead dog, its head shaved, was thrown through the window into Queen Mary's bedchamber. Prince Philip was a Catholic and a foreigner. It was not only Protestants who were full of apprehension, but Catholics, too, were sharply divided over the prospect of this alliance. It was widely believed that England would be given to Philip as a marriage dowry, and would sink into being a mere province of Spain. Nevertheless, Queen Mary was determined that the marriage should take place, and an ambassador was sent from Spain to conclude the marriage treaty.

The ambassador, Count Egmont, landed in Kent, and was badly received by the Kentish men, who would have torn him to pieces, as they at first believed he was the Queen's bridegroom. However, he arrived safely at Westminster and had an audience with the Queen, after which the articles of her marriage were communicated to the Lord Mayor and the City of London. The terms stipulated that Philip should aid Mary in governing her kingdom, a fact which did not escape her people's notice. The Spanish embassy slipped away discreetly by boat to Gravesend and left the country in chaos. The following week three insurrections broke out in different parts of England.

Christmas was spent quietly at Bradgate, in contrast to the celebrations and visits of the previous year. In the bleak and wintry days of January, Lady Katherine, overlooked and lonely, was unaware of the prevailing discord. Returning from a solitary ride she was surprised to find the forecourt of her father's house alive with horsemen. Sumpter mules were being laden with provisions, horses neighed, orders were shouted, men-at-arms hurried hither and thither, and all was bustle and confusion.

Indoors, she found her women huddled together, anxious and upset.

"What is to do?" she enquired, but nobody knew. If only Nelly were here, thought Katherine, she would soon find out what it was all about. She determined to find her mother, and was on the way to her solar when she encountered a young man called Adrian Stokes, who had just left it.

"What is happening?" Katherine enquired of him. "Where is my father, and what are all those men-at-arms about?"

"Madam," he replied, "the Duke of Suffolk is closeted with his brothers, the Lord Thomas Grey, and Lord John Grey."

"For what purpose?"

"Sir Thomas Wyatt has raised an army

in Kent, to rally those of the Protestant faith to restore the Lady Jane to the throne. The Duke, your father, and his brothers, have raised a company of horse and are about to join him."

"Restore Jane to the throne? Oh, no! What folly is this? Where is it to end?"

"In victory, we hope," replied the young man smoothly, and bowing, took his leave.

"But — but we have all sworn allegiance to Queen Mary," said Katherine, in bewilderment. "Poor Jane! Oh, my poor sister. Her one desire is to return home and live quietly with her books. What shall we do? Oh, what shall we do? What will happen to her?"

There was no one to answer this question.

The whole country was now in a state of confusion and uproar. Neighbour against neighbour, Catholic against Protestant, and Catholic against Catholic; supporters of Queen Mary turning against her over the issue of her marriage.

Treachery was rife. The Duke of Suffolk and his brothers, Lord Thomas

Grey and Lord John Grey, with a strong party of horse, took their way through Leicestershire, proclaiming the Lady Jane queen in every town through which they passed. The Duke of Huntingdon, who had promised to reinforce the Duke of Suffolk's army by enlisting his tenants in Ashby de la Zouche, instead reported Suffolk's plans to the Queen's Council. He was sent at the head of a force to capture Suffolk, who was expecting him as an ally. They met at Coventry, where the Duke of Suffolk's men were routed, but he and his brothers deserted, and escaped.

In the meantime, impeded by the appalling wintry conditions, Wyatt's army, bedraggled and storm-tossed, dragged their guns through the muddy lanes to reach London late one night in early February. Panic-stricken, its citizens locked themselves into their houses, allowing the army to pass through, unmolested, and attack Whitehall Palace at two o'clock in the morning. The palace was thrown into a state of confusion, the Queen's ladies crying and wringing their hands, running from room to room, and shrieking in terror. In that night of horror, every one lost their presence of mind but the queen, herself, who displayed the utmost courage, and at the most alarming crisis of the assault, stood in the gallery of the Gate-house of the palace, within arquebus-shot of the enemy to rally her supporters.

In the confusion and turmoil, the difficulty was to tell friend from foe, Wyatt's troops only being distinguished by their mud-stained apparel. With the war-cry 'Down with the draggle-tails' the queen's soldiers, encouraged by her bravery, defended fiercely, and gradually Wyatt's men were beaten back. Wyatt, himself, was forced down Fleet Street, where, exhausted, his spirit broken, he sat down on a fish-stall and allowed himself to be captured by an unarmed cavalier, who took him up on his back and carried him off to be imprisoned in the Tower.

The incredible uproar of this assault was plainly heard by the Tower's inmates, the firing of guns, shouting and screaming, mingling with the roars of the animals, disturbed, in the Tower lion-pit. Lady

Jane, awakening, listened, terrified, to what was to be her death knell.

Only a small bodyguard was left on the estate at Bradgate to look after the Duchess of Suffolk and her daughters. They lived in fear of their lives, daily expecting marauding soldiers, who at the least, would empty their larders, but at worst would rape and pillage and kill. At night the doors were bolted early, and those servants who were left took turns in mounting guard. Their overseer was the young man called Adrian Stokes, whom Lady Katherine had first encountered leaving her mother's solar. He was a handsome, auburn-haired man in his early twenties, whose duties, in normal times, were to look after the Duchess of Suffolk's horses.

In the absence of her husband, the Duchess leaned heavily on this young man. She soon discovered that he wrote a fair hand, and he became her secretary and major domo. Soon, the Duchess of Suffolk was seldom seen without him at her side. He was her constant companion. Nevertheless, Katherine was astonished, one day, upon entering her mother's solar, unannounced, to find her seated by the fire, Adrian Stokes on the floor by her side, his head in her lap, and she stroking his tawny curls.

The Lady Katherine stared, open-mouthed. It was the strangest sight to see her mother caressing anybody. The Duchess pushed the young man from her and rose hastily.

"Well," she demanded curtly to her daughter, "and what means this intrusion?"

Lady Katherine was saved from her mother's wrath by a sudden commotion outside. A servant entered the Duchess's apartment, followed closely by a small company of soldiers.

"Madam," said their leader, without preamble, "I beg leave to search your house."

"Search my house!" exclaimed the Duchess. "For what purpose, and by whose authority do you come here?"

"I am commanded by the Earl of Huntingdon to arrest your husband, the Duke of Suffolk, who has risen against her Grace, Queen Mary."

"The Earl of Huntingdon's orders! But

is he not on the side of the Protestants? I have heard my husband name him as an ally."

"My master is a loyal Englishman who fights for the Queen. And now, madam, I demand to know where your husband is hiding."

"He is not here."

"If you will not deliver him up to me, my men must search the house. I warn you, it would be better to lead us to him."

"I tell you he is not here."

The soldiers were ordered to search the house from top to bottom. Tapestries were torn from the walls, swords run through mattresses; closets were ransacked and the whole house reduced to chaos. The search was then continued in the park. The Duchess learned that her husband's forces had been put to rout at Coventry, by the Earl of Huntingdon, whom the duke had been relying upon as an ally. The Duke of Suffolk, himself and his brothers, had escaped, and it was thought that they had returned to Bradgate.

Even after dark, the soldiers continued

their search by lamplight, fruitlessly. Adrian Stokes and the few remaining servants had been guarded during this operation, but at nightfall they were locked up in one of the mansion's four towers. The Duchess of Suffolk and her two daughters were allowed to retire to bed, unmolested.

The soldiers remained, and settled down for the night on the rush-strewn floor of the hall. In the morning, the search was continued, so certain were the soldiers that somewhere on the estate the Duke lay hidden. Adrian Stokes and the servants were kept locked up; only the Duchess and her daughters were free to come and go as they wished. Perhaps the soldiers thought they would be led to the Duke by the indiscretion of his wife or one of his daughters. They huddled together miserably in the Duchess's solar, too distracted to occupy themselves, or even to try to reduce the destruction wrought by the marauders. The rich blue and silver arras lining the walls was slashed with sword cuts and hung all awry. The contents of a large oaken chest were scattered all over the floor. Upon a table was a platter of cold meat and some bread which the duchess herself had brought from the kitchen and which they pecked at desultorily. Looking at it, Lady Katherine was reminded of her pets, her pony, her monkey and her two spaniels. Who would feed them, since the servants were all under lock and key? And her mother's horses, would they have been given their hay?

"Madam," said Lady Katherine to her mother, "what of the animals? I must give them food and water, for there is nobody to look after them."

"It were wiser to stay together," said the duchess. "Surely these men will soon be satisfied that nobody is hiding here, and they will go."

But the search continued all that day and the men again settled down in the hall for the night. Next morning, when they again started to comb the estate, Lady Katherine was distracted.

"I *must* see to the needs of the animals," she said, and stopping only to wrap a warm cloak about herself she took what was left of the meat on the table, and left the chamber, in spite of her mother's protests. Outside the house were two men left on guard. They watched Katherine, but did not molest her, and as she sped across the pleasance towards the stables, one of them followed her.

She pushed open the stable door and entered, to be fallen upon by her dogs, who leapt upon her ecstatically, and all but knocked the platter of meat from her hand. She quietened them, and divided the meat into three portions, taking one to the cage in the corner of the stable, where Beppo was running up and down, chattering excitedly. She ladled out water from a large butt, watched all the time by the soldier, who stood by the open door, looking in.

Now Lady Katherine approached the horses, and saw that, as she had expected, their mangers were quite empty. Leaving the stable, she passed the watching soldier, her head held high, ignoring him. Her dogs, enjoying their freedom, ran round her, back and forth. At a little distance from the stable was a stackyard, and Katherine, entering this, made for a great pile of hay, loosely built, the soldier a yard or two behind her. One of the dogs scampered off nose to the ground, clearly on the track of rat or rabbit. The other one stayed with her, but as Katherine took a great bundle of hay into her arms, he ran round the stack, tail wagging, and started to scratch vigorously.

"Come on, sir, come on. You'll find nothing there," called Katherine, and started to walk back to the stables. The dog thought otherwise, refused to leave the stack, and continued to run round excitedly, scratching here and there. The soldier, instead of following Katherine, approached the haystack, and drawing his sword, plunged it in, first on one side, then the other. At his third plunge, there was a great howl of anguish, a scrabbling about, and the sudden appearance of a man's head, blood running down the cheek. Emerging from the stack, and confronted by the drawn sword, the man attempted to run, tripped up and lay upon the ground, straddled by the soldier, whose shouts soon brought others to the scene.

Katherine turned, dropped her hay, and ran back. The man lying upon the ground was dirty and dishevelled. Wisps of hay stuck to his face, and from a sword gash which had all but gouged out his eye, blood flowed freely.

"Uncle Thomas!" exclaimed Katherine, in consternation.

"'Tis Lord Thomas Grey!" cried one of the men. Katherine was pulled aside. "Here, get this dog out of the way," said a soldier, giving it a vicious kick. Katherine called off her dog, and watched horrified, as her uncle was roughly pulled to his feet, and dragged away, stumbling with exhaustion.

Stopping only to lock her dogs into the stable, Lady Katherine ran back to the house and burst into her mother's solar.

"They've caught Uncle Thomas!"

"What? Thomas? Where was he?"

"Hiding in a stack of hay. One of the dogs started scratching round it, then a soldier came up and thrust his sword through. He all but gouged out poor Uncle Thomas's eye."

"Where is he now?"

"They've taken him prisoner. Alack, poor Uncle Thomas, he could hardly walk. How long had he been hiding there, think you?"

"For two days, of a surety," said Lady Suffolk, then, "Where are your dogs now?"

"They are shut in the stable."

"Go fetch them indoors quickly."

"Why, Madam? They are comfortable and warm in their stable."

"Go at once, child. Who else might they not sniff out if they are released by the men."

"You mean — "

"I mean your father. If your Uncle Thomas was in hiding here, like as not your father is here, as well. Go, fetch your dogs, and quickly."

Katherine went, but not soon enough. Already, both spaniels had been released from the stables, and they were running about, this way and that, sniffling here, scratching there, tails wagging, enjoying their new game, egged on by the soldiers.

There was nothing that Katherine could do, but watch helplessly. And even as she watched, one of them bounded up to a hollow tree, barking joyfully. The searchers surrounded it, and discovered the Duke of Suffolk, who had crouched there, foodless and shivering with cold, for two whole days. He stumbled out, half-dead, cold and cramped, and collapsed at the feet of the seekers. Within an hour they were on their way to London, bearing with them triumphantly, their two prisoners.

Before they departed, Adrian Stokes and the servants were released, and the captain of the band apologized perfunctorily to the duchess for the inconvenience he had caused her.

In London Queen Mary, who had pardoned the Grey family, and been willing to release her usurper, Lady Jane, the little cousin of whom she had been fond, was at last convinced of their perfidy. She rode through the city, past the gruesome sight of many corpses dangling at their own front doors, deserters from her standard during the rebellion. At Temple Bar, on a spot saturated with the blood of her subjects, she was persuaded, on the plea that such scenes would be frequent while she suffered the competitor for her throne to exist, to sign a warrant specifying that Lady Jane and her husband Guildford Dudley were to be executed immediately.

Lady Jane Grey was ready to die. Her last messages had been written and dispatched. Among them was a letter, written on the blank pages of her Greek Testament, and sent to her sister Katherine. It was a long letter, serene and unworldly. Lady Katherine read it and re-read it, convulsed with grief for the sister who was to endure so violent a death but lost in admiration for her calm fortitude.

Once Lady Katherine had seen a chicken beheaded, and watched with fascinated horror the headless body take its last few jerky steps, blood pouring from it, before the scullion grabbed it by its feet, and holding it upside down, started to pluck the feathers from its still-flapping wings.

Today her sister Jane's head was to be chopped off her delicate white neck for no crime other than obedience, obedience to her parents and to her father-in-law. For their folly, their greed and treachery, Northumberland had already paid the price, and her father and uncles were in prison, awaiting execution. But Jane was their innocent catspaw. It was all wrong that she should die as well. Queen Mary had been fond of her, had sent her gifts, such a short time ago. Surely she would not allow her little cousin to die so violently. Katherine remembered suddenly the necklace of rubies and pearls that Mary had sent to Jane, and how the flickering candlelight had made it seem like drops of blood dripping down her neck.

And now, today, the axe would fall, would sever her head from her body. Suppose the headsman's axe should miss, should fail to kill her cleanly at his first blow. Katherine clutched her own neck in an agony of concern for her sister. Through her tears she read and re-read Jane's letter and was comforted. She wrote,

> *'I have sent you, good sister Katherine, a book, which, though it be not outwardly trimmed with gold, yet inwardly it is of more worth than precious stones. It is the book, dear sister, of the laws of the Lord; it is*

His Testament and last Will, which he bequeathed to us poor wretches, which shall lead us to the path of eternal joy; and if you, with good mind and an earnest desire, follow it, it will bring you to immortal and everlasting life. It will teach you to live, it will teach you to die.'

How could she have written with such serenity? It was almost as though she had already passed from this world, had left behind its vanities and sorrows.

The letter finished,

'As touching my death, rejoice as I do, and consider that I shall be delivered from corruption and put on incorruption, for I am assured that I shall for losing a mortal life find an immortal felicity. Pray God grant that ye live in His fear and die in His love, neither for love of life nor fear of death. Farewell, dear sister; put your only trust in God, who only must uphold you.
Your loving sister, Jane Dudley.'

Outside, on this bleak and cheerless February day, the fine trees along the carriageway leading to the house, were being beheaded, pollarded in anguish for Lady Jane, by one of the gamekeepers.

Nurse Ellen's duties at the Tower of London were concluded after she had attended her young mistress to the scaffold. She returned to Bradgate, distraught.

"She died so bravely," sobbed the old nurse, "walking to the scaffold, her prayer book in her hand, as serenely as though she were walking to church; and that only half an hour after she had stood at her prison window and watched her husband's body wheeled past in a handcart."

"She saw Guildford after he was beheaded?" whispered Katherine, horrified.

"That she did, his head wrapped in a bloody cloth beside his body, then she walked out to her own death without a tremor."

"Oh, she was brave."

"She seemed almost glad to die, madam, to be done with it all."

"I think she was. Poor Jane."

"They tried to turn her to thc Catholic faith at the end, but t'was no use. They do say Queen Mary would have pardoned her after all if she had recanted. But she stood firm by her faith. The Queen sent her own confessor, Dr Feckenham to try to change her heart, but she had an answer to all his arguments. He was so troubled for her that he asked leave to accompany her to the scaffold when he saw it was useless to try to change her mind."

"Did she let him?"

"Aye, they knelt together at the end and said her favourite psalm: '*Have mercy upon me, O God, after Thy great goodness*'. She said it right through to the end, off by heart, and he followed her in Latin."

"They knelt down together, Nelly, Protestant and Catholic?"

"Aye, madam."

"And then they chopped her head off. I don't understand. It doesn't make sense to me."

The old woman was too choked to reply. But after a few minutes she went on, "She gave me her handkerchief and gloves, and then began to untie her cape herself. I was too overcome to help her, poor lady."

"And then, Nelly?"

"There she was, her neck and shoulders all exposed to the biting wind. The executioner knelt down before her and said, 'Do you forgive me, madam?' and she said poor little dear, 'most willingly,' then I pushed a kerchief into her hand, and she tied it over her own eyes."

Nurse Ellen was unable to continue. She was shaken with sobs. Katherine put an arm around her shoulders to comfort her. "And then, Nelly?"

"He said, 'Stand upon the straw, madam'. We couldn't help her. Nobody could lift a hand to guide her. She said, 'I pray you — despatch me quickly. Will you take it off before I lay me down?' He said, 'no, Madam.' She put out her hands, stumbling and crying, 'where is it, where is it?' And we stood there, we just stood there, and nobody lifted a finger to help her. We were all that overcome, not one of us could lead her to the block."

"Oh, poor Jane! My poor sister! What did she do?"

"She stumbled over the straw, and she cried out, 'What shall I do, what shall I do?' And still none of us could move. It was as though we were all paralysed. And there she stood alone, blindfolded, her poor naked shoulders exposed to the raw winter's wind, and I couldn't, I couldn't lead her to that wicked block. I couldn't do it, madam, no more could the others that were with her on that scaffold."

"And then, Nelly?" whispered Katherine through her tears.

"There were some people there, watching, and they began to protest, and then one of them, he climbed up and guided Lady Jane towards the block. It was a kindness to her, because none of us was able to help her. Then she knelt down and stretched out her arms, and the executioner raised his axe over her little, white neck, and she said out loud for everybody to hear, 'Lord, into Thy hands I commend my spirit.' Then down came the axe, and off came her head, and there was a great spurt of blood all over the straw. The executioner picked up her head, and held it aloft, and cried, 'So perish all the Queen's enemies! Behold the head of a traitor!'"

6

BRADGATE PARK, formerly the scene of bustling activity, was deserted except for a few servants, Lady Katherine and her little sister, Lady Mary. The Duke of Suffolk, imprisoned in the Tower, awaited execution, as did his brothers. The Duchess of Suffolk was away hunting, with her constant companion, Adrian Stokes. The house, devastated by the soldiers in their search for its master remained unkempt and neglected. Only Nurse Ellen maintained her authority, presiding over the nursery, and keeping a strict eye on little Lady Mary. Lady Mary was but nine years old, very small in stature, with a slightly crooked back. She was a quiet, gentle little girl who had worshipped her elder sister, Jane, but had been little noticed by Katherine. Now the two sisters were drawn together by loneliness, the disasters which had overtaken their family, and the uncertainty of their present position.

A fortnight after Lady Jane's execution, her father suffered the same fate, on the same day as Thomas Wyatt was executed. The confessions of that gentleman, before his death, implicated the queen's half-sister, the gay and lovely Elizabeth, who had ridden with Mary in her triumphal entrance to the city. Influenced by Renard, the Spanish ambassador in London, the Queen had Elizabeth imprisoned in the Tower.

Lord John Grey was released from prison on payment of a heavy fine, but three weeks after the Duke of Suffolk's death, his brother Thomas was also executed.

The following day, Lady Suffolk returned to Bradgate. She lost no time in summoning Lady Katherine and Lady Mary to her solar. Adrian Stokes was, as usual, by her side. They were both dressed in black, but it was not funereal black. Adrian Stokes wore a velvet doublet, ermine-trimmed and flashing with jewels, his red curls carefully pomaded. The duchess was equally bedecked and trimmed, in black satin and ermine, gems in her hair and rich chains and carcanets about her neck. But against the slim elegance of her escort, her once fine figure looked fat and gross, her complexion florid. She fingered the chains about her neck, and her daughters saw on one of her plump white hands two wedding rings.

"This is my husband," the duchess said without preamble, "for Adrian and I were married this day."

Katherine and Mary were too much astonished to say anything, and the duchess continued, "Your father's estates have been confiscated. It is necessary for us all to leave Bradgate immediately."

"Leave Bradgate!" cried Lady Katherine. Where shall we go?"

"I shall live with my husband," continued the duchess imperturbably, "but her Grace, Queen Mary, has indicated her willingness to receive you both at court."

"We are to go to court?"

"Yes, as maids of honour to the Queen."

"I don't understand. Our family is in disgrace with the Queen, and she has caused the deaths of Jane and father and Uncle Thomas. Yet you say we are to go to court to serve her! What mean you?"

"The Queen bears no malice towards you or towards me. She was obliged for reasons of state to do what she did. You must accept her patronage with a good grace, for there is none other to provide for you now."

Bewildered, Katherine stood staring at her mother, speechless.

"Go now, and make your preparations for departure. Two days hence, we shall all be off."

"My animals," faltered Katherine.

"Take them, by all means. The Queen's palace is large. Doubtless they can be accommodated." With an airy wave of her plump hand, the Duchess of Suffolk dismissed her daughters.

Lady Katherine and her little sister at once sought out Mrs Ellen, their pillar of strength. That good woman apprised of the situation, was already sorting and packing her charges' wardrobes.

"You know what is to become of us, Nelly?"

"Aye," said the old woman grimly,

shaking out a satin petticoat.

Spread out upon thc bcd was Lady Katherine's wedding dress of gold and silver brocade, embroidered with precious gems. She looked at it and sighed. Less than a year ago she had worn that beautiful gown, standing by the side of her sister, Jane. Sad they had been, unwilling brides both. How much sadder they would have been, had they foreseen the turn of events. And what did the future hold? Was the queen in truth benevolently inclined towards them, in spite of all the treachery of their relations?

The following day, the long journey to London was begun. Muffled up against the keen March wind, Lady Katherine travelled by horseback, little Lady Mary, in charge of Beppo the monkey, and the two spaniels, with Nurse Ellen, in a horse litter. They were followed by their maids and men servants and sumpter horses loaded with all their possessions.

It was hard going, for the roads were full of ruts, and soft with mud and melted snow. The horses stumbled their way through the slush, and had only completed half the journey by nightfall. They came to an inn where they might rest for the night. Mrs Ellen was anxious for her charges.

"My lady," she said anxiously, "'twere best not to divulge who you are. These are troubled times, and folks divided in their allegiances. Some for the Queen, some against her, but 'tis best not to bruit abroad that you are the kinswoman of Queen Jane."

"You are right, good Nelly," agreed Lady Katherine and sent in her man with a request for lodgings for Dame Hardwick, the first name that came into her head.

Since they were obviously ladies of quality, the innkeeper gave the two sisters a good room to themselves attended by Mrs Ellen, whilst their servants made shift for themselves, and settled down among the rushes in the common room. The inn-keeper's wife brought steaming bowls of frumenty, served with generous portions of honey, and a maid aired the great four-poster bed with a brass warming-pan. They were ready to gossip about the troubled times.

"Even the bairns are divided," said the innkeeper's wife, and described how a large company of children, playing on some waste ground, on the outskirts of the town, had formed themselves into two bands, to play the game 'the Queen against Wyatt'. They fought so vigorously that several were seriously wounded, and the urchin who played Prince Philip, the queen's intended spouse, being taken prisoner and hanged, was nearly throttled in good earnest, before some good people, passing by, intervened and had him cut down.

Instructions were given to have the horses ready early the next morning, and so soon as it was light the little cavalcade was on its way. Conditions soon became worse than the previous day, for sleet began to fall and a keen east wind blew into the riders' eyes and noses. As the day wore on Lady Katherine became numbed and exhausted. Huddled into her hood she could scarce see where she was going, as her horse stumbled on. Nor did she care. She longed only for this journey to end, to feel warmth and comfort again. But night had fallen before the muddy lanes were left behind, and the horses's hooves at last rang out on the cobbled streets of London. The towers of Westminster loomed up before them, piercing the darkness of the sky.

Here, in contrast to the lonely country roads, all was noise and bustle. A great courtyard was lit by flares which shone upon scullions, soldiers, courtiers, grooms and lackeys all about their business.

Lady Katherine dismounted, and almost collapsed with stiffness, fatigue and cold. But the journey was over. She and her little sister, Mary, were escorted to the Maidens' Chamber, and went to bed at once.

The next day, Queen Mary sent for Lady Katherine. Rested and refreshed, and clad in a kirtle of blue velvet, over a petticoat of gleaming pink taffeta, her golden curls escaping from a tippet of fine lace, many an eye was turned upon her approvingly as she was led through a bewildering maze of corridors and staircases, halls and galleries, to the Queen's presence. But she felt some apprehension as she entered Queen Mary's chamber, remembering the regal figure she had cut, at the head of a magnificent cavalcade of ladies and gentlemen when she had entered London to claim her throne; that throne which had been usurped by Katherine's sister Jane, and for which she and her father and uncle had paid with their lives.

Queen Mary was seated informally by her fireside, surrounded by her ladies and was intent upon a piece of intricate embroidery. Katherine made a deep curtsey and remained with bent knee and downcast eyes, until a kindly voice said, "Get up, child, and let me have a look at you."

She raised her eyes and saw a plump little middle-aged lady with a plain but pleasant countenance, not the face of a despotic ruler or a ruthless executioner.

"M-m, you have grown quite a comely lass," appraised Queen Mary, "now what shall we do with you?" Her eyes returned to her embroidery, and she began matching up some silk threads to her pattern, with such absorption that Lady Katherine began to wonder whether she was forgotten or had been dismissed. Should she make her curtsey and withdraw, or should she wait to be dismissed? She looked about her, distrait, and noticed one of the queen's ladies regarding her with some interest. She had a beautiful, if somewhat delicate face, with enormous dark eyes. Katherine returned her look, wondering where she had seen that face before.

Queen Mary laid down her embroidery and said decisively, "We will put you and your young sister in the charge of the Duchess of Somerset."

Katherine was delighted. She could hardly believe her ears, for the Duchess of Somerset was none other than Lord Hertford's mother.

"Here is her daughter, Lady Jane Seymour," and the Queen indicated the lady who had already attracted Katherine's attention. Of course, she was Ned Hertford's sister, and remarkably like him, in a gentler, more feminine way. Queen Mary continued, "She will tell you your duties and be a sister to you, will you not, Lady Jane?"

It was an unfortunate phrase, bringing to Katherine's mind at once the memory of her sister Jane. Her eyes filled with tears.

"With great pleasure," agreed Lady Jane Seymour, looking at Katherine sympathetically.

The Queen dismissed them.

"I shall never find my way about," sighed Katherine bewildered by the many twists and turns as Jane Seymour led her back to a small sitting-room leading from the Maidens' Chamber, which she was privileged to call her own.

"Of course you will, in no time at all," comforted her guide. "Now we can have a good talk," she said cheerfully, indicating a low stool for Katherine and settling herself down on another.

"You are fond of my brother Ned?" she asked at once without preamble.

The colour flooded in to Katherine's face as she answered simply, "Yes."

"He has spoken of you often to me."

"He has?" cried Katherine, delightedly.

"He told me how you saved his life from a wolf."

Katherine sighed. So long ago that enchanted night seemed now, another life. Now she was another person, no longer a carefree child, but an orphan and a discarded wife, her father dead and discredited, her mother re-married to a man who was half her age, her sister executed. She and her little sister Mary, the dwarf, were like pieces of driftwood, salvaged by Queen Mary from their sea of disasters, but not belonging anywhere any more.

"Don't be so sad. You will be happy here. And soon my brother Ned is coming to court. That will please you, won't it?"

Katherine smiled. She was very gratified by the obvious interest which Lady Jane Seymour was taking in her. She was several years older than Katherine, being in her twentieth year, occupied a position of some authority in the Queen's establishment, was beautiful and charming, but above all, she was Lord Hertford's sister.

Under Lady Jane's guidance Lady Katherine soon fell into the court routine and did all that was required of her including her attendance at Mass every morning. Although she had been brought up as a devout Protestant and still thought of herself as one, she had no scruples about attending a Catholic Mass as part of her official duties. What to her sister, Jane, had been a heresy which she was ready to give her life to deny, was to Lady Katherine merely a ritual to be recited.

It was a sober atmosphere which surrounded Queen Mary, with lengthy prayers every evening, pious readings and telling of beads. There was little opportunity for levity, nevertheless the maids and the young courtiers, led by the two prettiest and boldest of all the queen's ladies, Lady Jane Dormer and Lettice Knollys, found a place of complete freedom where court etiquette was relaxed and piety abolished. This was in some rooms above the water-gate, belonging to Lettice's cousin, Master Keyes. He was the Queen's Sergeant Porter and was responsible for all who came and went by way of the river, as most people did; also all rioters and brawlers in the palace precincts were delivered over for castigation by his grooms. He was well suited to this post, for he was a mountain of a man calculated to strike terror into the heart of any wrong-doer. He stood six feet seven in his hose and was as broad as a house. But he was, in fact, a very gentle giant, a widower in his middle age. Lettice would act as hostess to the afternoon parties he loved to give. Through his bow windows cool breezes blew off the Thames, and the young people about the court made free of his apartments, and munched his marchpanes and sipped his canary, while one of their number would play the virginal or lute or mandoline.

One of the most frequent visitors to Master Keyes' apartments was Lady Katherine's little sister, Lady Mary, and a warm if somewhat incongruous friendship sprang up between the giant and the dwarf. She would sit for hours at his window, fascinated by the river traffic; by the ships sailing up the Thames from all over the world, with their cargoes of silks and spices and precious gems; by the constant coming and going of ladies and courtiers in gaily painted and festooned barges; and by the graceful swans adorning the river. Here Lady Katherine would join little Lady

Mary when her duties permitted, for they had come close together since the disintegration of their family, and Lady Katherine felt a responsibility towards her little sister.

They were thus engaged, watching the ships sail past, when somebody entered the room. Katherine turned, and there was Lord Hertford, a smile upon his lips.

"Ned!"

"Kate, my dear Kate!"

"I am so happy to see you, so very happy."

"And I you. You have made a conquest of my sister Jane. She talks of nobody but you."

"Lady Jane has been so kind to me, and I admire her very much."

"So you are a lady-in-waiting to the Queen. And how do you enjoy court life?"

"Very well indeed, at this moment. I could not be happier," Katherine replied.

Their tête-à-tête was interrupted by the entrance of Thomas Keyes bearing in his hand a placard.

"Look here," he said. "This has just

been thrown through one of the kitchen windows and it landed in a great bowl of dough which was proving on the table."

Katherine laughed and Ned said, "A good shot. Doubtless thrown by some apprentice. What does it say?"

"It is no laughing matter. The placard says '*Death to the bastard if she weds the Prince of Spain*'."

"Feelings are still running high over the Queen's intended marriage," said Hertford. "Did you hear about the haunted house in Aldersgate Street?"

"The haunted house?"

"Yes, I was riding by when I saw great crowds of people thronging round it to hear a ghostly voice. When somebody shouted 'God save Queen Mary' the voice was silent. But if the people cried 'God save the Lady Elizabeth', it answered 'So be it'. If they asked, 'What is the Mass?' it answered 'Idolatry'."

"Whose was this voice?" asked Katherine in astonishment.

"The voice of an angel inveighing against the queen's marriage," answered Hertford, "according to the people, and they were greatly excited. A strange matter, but I cannot tell you how it ended for I could not stop. I was already late for my game of tennis, but as I rode away I heard the people cry 'The angel speaks again'."

"Some angel it was, too," said Master Keyes, taking up the story, "for it proved to be Bess the harlot, who had been hidden in the wall."

"How was she discovered?"

"The disturbance went on until the council ordered that the wall from whence the voice issued should be pulled down, and there she was. She confessed that she had been hired to inflame the mob, and she was set in the pillory for a punishment. But nothing worse befell her since her employers were to blame and they could not be discovered."

"It's a sorry matter, this marriage the queen is so set upon," said Hertford.

"Aye, 'tis said there was a conspiracy to kill Queen Mary as she walked in St James's Park."

"How so?"

"By means of a burning glass fixed on the leads of a neighbouring house."

Hertford laughed. "A far-fetched

scheme," he said, "but there may be others more likely to succeed."

"Aye, 'tis so. And all those around Her Majesty are at risk," said Master Keyes. "A pity the Queen is so set upon this match."

But set upon the marriage Queen Mary was, and nothing would deter her from it. Negotiations proceeded between England and Spain, and in due course Count Egmont returned, on especial embassy, bearing a betrothal ring from King Philip of Spain. Queen Mary had been expecting him daily, and had worked herself up to a great state of agitation, fearing that King Philip would think again about the projected marriage.

When Count Egmont was escorted into her presence by the Earl of Pembroke, the eucharist was in the apartment. The Queen dropped upon her knees before it, and clasping her hands, declared with great pathos that her sole object in the marriage was the good of her kingdom. Her emotion communicated itself to the ladies around her, and there was not a dry eye as the oaths confirming the marriage were taken on the part of England and Spain. Then all the company knelt together to pray that God would bless the marriage.

Queen Mary was then presented with a very handsome ring that the King of Spain had sent her, and the Count of Egmont took his departure. The Queen could not take her eyes off the ring, and displayed it continually with great pride.

7

THE Queen's forthcoming marriage now became the chief topic of conversation among her ladies, who discussed endlessly the gowns they would wear, and the partners they hoped to captivate at the balls and festivities attendant on the wedding. All except Lady Jane Seymour, who was pale and wan. Partly out of true concern for her friend and partly from a desire to make some further contact with Lord Hertford, Lady Katherine decided to seek him out. But it was easier said than done. Ned Hertford came and went like a will-o'-the-wisp, often deserting the court for long periods, and Katherine began to despair of seeing him. At last, Jane Seymour herself begged Katherine to tell Ned of her indisposition. She had taken to her bed and was being visited by Katherine, when she said, "Write a note for me, to tell my brother I am ill. Give it to my man, and he will deliver it to Cannon Street, whcre Ned has a place. My man knows the place well."

Katherine obeyed her friend at once and awaited Ned's arrival with some impatience.

He came without delay in answer to his sister's summons, and after visiting her, sought out Katherine.

"I fear my sister is quite ill," he said. "Jane has always been delicate, and town air does not suit her. It is so hot and sultry now, and London stinks. To tell the truth, I myself often long for the pure air of Hanworth, where my mother has a house. How would it be if I use Jane's indisposition as an excuse for all three of us to leave court and stay at Hanworth for a recreation?"

"All three of us? You mean me, too?"

"Why not? Would you not care to come with us?"

"Indeed, yes, but would the Queen permit it?"

"She is so happy in her betrothal to the Spaniard that she will permit anything."

As a matter of fact Lady Jane Seymour now became so alarmingly ill with a high fever that the Queen decided she must go home at once. She was placed in a palanquin, a litter borne by men, and conveyed to Hanworth in the care of the mother of the maids. The Queen readily gave permission for Lord Hertford and Lady Katherine Grey to accompany Lady Jane, and they followed on horseback, Katherine a pretty enough picture in her riding habit of green velvet, her cheeks bright with the exercise and the fresh air, her red-gold curls tumbled beneath her hood.

Katherine was happy as she rode by Ned's side; happy to be free for a while from the etiquette and restrictions of court life; happy to be riding through the countryside on a summer's day through lanes bright with poppies and mallow and ragged robin; but happiest of all to be by the side of her beloved Ned. And he, not insensible of Katherine's charms, was as gallant an escort as any maid could wish for. It was fortunate for poor Lady Jane that the mother of the maids was in attendance on her, for Lady Katherine had completely forgotten her friend's indisposition, as she chatted gaily with Ned.

The journey tried Lady Jane sorely, and she was put to bed as soon as she arrived at her mother's house. She stayed there for some three or four weeks, dosed with simples and herbs and medicines until the fever abated. Lady Katherine was not required at her friend's bedside. Indeed, she found herself somewhat in the way there, as Lady Jane was too ill for social visits, and had much attention from her mother's maidservants. So Katherine and Ned were thrown upon each other's company, and had soon established the old cameraderie which they had enjoyed at Bradgate when Katherine was a child. They rode together, played bowls, and sang duets in the evenings. Lady Katherine was blissfully happy. Their growing intimacy was, however, looked upon with some consternation by Lady Somerset. It was not that she disliked Katherine. Indeed, her lightheartedness and beauty added life and colour to Hanworth, which had been somewhat subdued since the execution of its master, Lord Somerset. But Lady Somerset, having been reinstated at court, and had her husband's estates restored to her, was anxious to remain in the Queen's favour, and had no wish for her son to be mixed up with this unfortunate Grey family, charming as Lady Katherine undoubtedly was.

One day Hertford had disappeared on business of his own, and Katherine repaired to a favourite spot beneath a weeping willow, by the side of an ornamental lake. There was plenty to divert her. She watched a proud mallard duck waddle to the lake followed by her brood, hardly dry from the eggs she had just hatched. One after another they half-flew, half-fell into the water and were at once completely at home in it, paddling away from the mother duck in ever widening circles until a warning quack from her brought them scudding back. There were moorhens here, and swallows dipping over the water. The air was scented with meadow-sweet and Katherine drowsed contentedly upon the mossy bank. She was startled awake by a series of furious quacks, followed by peeping, and saw to her consternation one of the moorhens holding a duckling under the water with its beak. Katherine threw a twig, then another and another, hurtling them into the water with more haste than accuracy. Although she succeeded in frightening the moorhen away she was too late to save the duckling, who floated lifelessly, a little bedraggled blob upon the water.

"Hey, what's to-do?" cried a voice behind Katherine, and there was Ned, laughing at Katherine's distraction.

"Oh, Ned, look, poor little thing, it's only just hatched out, and it's dead already. What a wicked, futile waste of life."

"Some of them have to die, Kate. There'd be far too many otherwise."

"What is the point of it all? So soon as our backs are turned that spiteful moorhen will be back, and it'll kill another and another, and soon the duck won't have any left. She was so proud bringing them down to the water but she hasn't got a chance to look after them."

"Nature is cruel and ruthless and wasteful, Kate."

"Life is cruel. Cruel and pointless," said Katherine.

The duckling's death brought back to her memory all the unhappiness and disruption of her past life; her sister Jane's execution, and her father's and uncle's. The tranquility of the past few weeks was shattered for her. How could she have been so happy in so cruel a world? Her tears began to flow.

"Oh, come now, Kate sweetheart. All that grief for one duckling? It's dead now. It's troubles are over. And as for the mother duck, she's quite content with what she has left. Ducks can't count, you know. Come, let me see you smile."

"It's not the duckling, Ned. It — it's everything. Jane, poor Jane — chopping off her head. How awful it all was. Did you know she saw Guildford, dead, just before they took her to the scaffold?"

"No, I didn't know that. Poor Jane. How was that?"

"She watched him go to the scaffold from her prison window, and she was still there waiting when they wheeled his body back in a handcart, his head separate, wrapped in a kerchief."

They fell silent, imagining the horror Jane must have felt.

"Did you love her, Ned? Did you love my sister Jane? She was going to be your wife once."

"I was very fond of Jane. Who wouldn't be? She was gentle and good and clever, but strong as well, like steel. 'Tis said Queen Mary would have granted a reprieve, had she but turned to the Catholic faith, but not Jane. Nothing would move her. She was too good for me, and too clever, alas.

"Not like you, Kate. You're not clever, are you?" He was gently teasing now. "But you're sweet, little Kate, and so pretty."

He put his arm round her and her head leaned against his shoulder. She was not crying now. Gently he turned her face towards him and pressed his lips to hers.

"Hoity-toity, here's a fine to-do!"

Kate and Ned sprang apart and found the Duchess of Somerset regarding them. "When I came down to the water," she said, "to see if the mallard had hatched her clutch, I did not expect to find my son taking liberties with my charge."

"You do me wrong, madam. I take no

liberty with the Lady Katherine."

"No liberty?"

"I love her. Do you hear me? I love Lady Katherine."

"What is that you say?"

"I love Kate, and I want her for my wife. It's true, Mother."

The Duchess of Somerset was hardly more surprised than Lord Hertford was, when he heard himself declare his love for Katherine. As for Lady Katherine, she was as astonished and delighted as the old duchess was concerned and anxious.

"There will be much ado when the Queen hears of this," she said grimly.

"Why should there be? The Queen is full of good-will towards me. She gave me permission to come here with my sister, knowing Katherine was coming too, so she cannot object to us being together. Surely young folks meaning well may enjoy each other's company."

"Not without her Majesty's approval."

"I will get it so soon as we return to London."

"Do that, my son," said his mother uneasily.

Now all the warmth of Katherine's ardent nature became centred upon Ned, 'her sweet lord', and Hertford, flattered by her adoration, and admiring her wildrose beauty, was soon as much in love with her as she with him. Lady Jane was delighted that her friend was to become her sister-in-law, and even Lady Somerset's misgivings were stilled by the happiness of the young people.

Lady Jane Seymour was strong and well again, and so Lord Hertford escorted his sister and Lady Katherine back to court, all of them full of optimism for the future. Katherine and Ned were determined to ask the Queen's permission to marry at the first opportunity. But they found the court in a great flurry of excitement over the imminent arrival of Prince Philip of Spain, and the right moment for Hertford to approach Queen Mary never seemed to come.

The Queen decided that her nuptials should be celebrated at Winchester and there was much speculation among the young ladies in the maidens' bower as to whom would be chosen to accompany her.

"Mirror, mirror on the wall, who is the fairest of us all?" cried Lettice Knollys, a very handsome young woman.

"Why should she take the fairest of us?" enquired Lady Dormer.

"To impress her bridegroom, naturally."

"Nonsense, she'll take the plainest ones in the court."

"But why?"

"Because the Queen is middle-aged and plain," replied Lady Jane Dormer, with more candour than kindness. "She will not wish her bridegroom's eyes to rest too long on her attendants."

"That excludes me, then," giggled Lettice.

"And me, and me," chorused the rest of the maidens, conscious of their own charms.

There was great merriment in the bower until the mother of the maids appeared, clucking her disapproval of the noise her charges were making.

"It can be heard in every corner of the palace," she declared. "Now get off to bed, every one of you."

Katherine, unlike the rest of the maidens hoped desperately that she would be left behind so that she and Ned might not be parted; but the Queen decided otherwise, and both Katherine and Jane Seymour were among the ladies chosen to accompany the Queen.

Her Majesty had ordered a splendid wooden wagon to be made especially for this occasion. It was covered with fine red cloth, fringed with red silk, and lined with red buckram. Outside it was painted red to match, and the horses' collars, draughts, and reins were of red leather. The hammercloth, which covered and hung down from the driver's seat, bore the Queen's arms.

Before they departed upon their journey, this carriage had to be seen and admired by those ladies and gentlemen who were to be left behind. Although so gay and flamboyant, in truth the wagon was a high and clumsy vehicle, difficult for a lady to enter or leave. It was not really surprising, therefore, when one of the Queen's ladies, pretty little Lady Arabella Mewtas, stumbled as she was leaving the carriage and turned her ankle over. The pain was so acute that she would have swooned had not a courtier at her side seen her sway and adroitly caught her in his arms just as she was about to fall to the ground. The young man was Lord Hertford, and Lady Katherine's last sight of him was as he carried Arabella Mewtas away, his face full of concern for her. Katherine took this picture with her throughout the long journey, and the further they progressed from London, the more gloomy she became. At last they arrived at Farnham Castle, where they were to stay.

Queen Mary was in a fever of impatience as she awaited news of Prince Philip's arrival. She had sent Lord Admiral Howard with the finest ships of her navy, to join the Spanish fleet to escort Don Philip to his bride with the utmost maritime pomp.

In due course the tidings arrived that the prince and the combined fleets of England and Spain, amounting to one hundred and sixty-nine sail had made the port of Southampton.

A great concourse of nobles and gentry waited to receive him. And crowding behind was a huge mass of people, eager to watch the show. They were not disappointed, for the Queen had sent a magnificent state barge to meet her spouse. It was manned by twenty men dressed in Mary's liveries of green and white. The barge was lined with rich tapestry and the prince's seat covered with gold brocade. Twenty other barges followed, all lined with striped cloth, to accommodate Philip's officers of state.

The prince alighted at the mole, where he was immediately presented with the order of the garter, which the Earl of Arundel buckled below his knee, and he was invested with a mantle of blue velvet fringed with gold and pearls. The Queen had also sent a fine steed which the prince mounted and rode to the church of the Holy Rood in Southampton, to return thanks for his safe voyage. He was then conducted to a fine palace where an apartment had been made ready for him to spend the night.

All this pomp and ceremony was marred only by the conduct of the English sailors, who subjected their Spanish counterparts to jostling, jeering and brawling in the most unmannerly way. And the weather, which had been still and sunny, now changed, so that the Queen and her retinue set out towards Winchester in a furious storm of rain and wind, for nothing would persuade Her Majesty to delay the meeting with her prince.

The weather continued very stormy and it was still pouring with rain next morning when Prince Philip and his suite set out from Southampton in great state and solemn cavalcade for Winchester. The Earl of Pembroke had arrived to escort him, with two hundred and fifty cavaliers, superbly mounted, dressed in black velvet, and wearing heavy gold chains; behind them one hundred archers on horseback, dressed in yellow cloth striped with red velvet, their bows ready. And following the procession, at least four thousand spectators, variously mounted, defying the weather.

The Spanish Prince was protected from the rain by a red felt cloak and large black hat, but when he arrived at Winchester he threw off his heavy cloak, and was revealed in a purple velvet doublet and hose, richly embroidered with gold. He entered the city in great state on a fair white courser, to a volley of artillery.

The marriage was to take place the following day, but that night Don Philip went without ceremony, and on foot, from the Dean of Winchester's house, where he was staying, by a secret passage to the bishop's palace, where Queen Mary awaited him. She received him lovingly and conversed with him familiarly in Spanish for about half an hour. Before he left she playfully taught him to say in English, "Goodnight, my lords, all of you," which he learnt well enough to astonish the lords of the council who escorted him back to the deanery.

The day appointed for the royal nuptials was the twenty-fifth of July, the festival of St James, the patron saint of Spain. The royal couple vied with each other in the magnificence of their apparel. The bridegroom was dressed in a robe of rich brocade, bordered with large pearls and diamonds; his trunk-hose were of white satin, worked with silver. He wore a collar of beaten gold, full of priceless diamonds, from which hung the jewel of the Golden Fleece; at his knee was the

Garter, studded with beautiful coloured gems.

His bride walked on foot from the episcopal palace, attended by her principal nobility and ladies. She wore a robe richly brocaded on a gold ground, with a long train splendidly bordered with pearls and diamonds of great size. Her coif was bordered with two rows of large diamonds. Her kirtle beneath the robe was of white satin, wrought with silver. On her breast she wore an enormous diamond of inestimable value, sent to her as a gift from Philip while he was still in Spain. She was scintillating, but, not satisfied, the Queen insisted on scarlet boots.

The ceremonial in the Cathedral lasted from eleven in the morning until three in the afternoon, after which the bridal party adjourned to the hall in the bishop's palace, which was all hung with rich arras striped with gold and green. Here, a sumptuous banquet awaited them, the royal couple being seated upon a stately dais, and their table served with plate of solid gold. In a gallery a band of musicians played, their music being interspersed with congratulatory orations and panegyrics. Below the dais were spread tables, where the Queen's ladies, the English nobility, and the Spanish grandees with their wives, were feasted.

At length the banquet was over, the tables taken up, and dancing began. The Spanish ladies were forced to sit out as they did not know any English dances, but they were persuaded to perform a fandango, which showed off their very curious apparel. One of the most spectacular ladies was the Duchess of Alva. She was a very large and tall woman, attired in a gigantic farthingale. Her huge petticoat was embroidered in a design of parrots and squirrels pecking at cherries and oranges and other fruits, and even nuts; the whole on a ground of gold thread, worn in conjunction with a formidable ruff of gold lace and a headdress so peculiar as to baffle description.

At last the festivities came to an end. Queen Mary's ladies, tired but excited, relaxed in the privacy of the maidens' bower.

"So, ladies, our Queen has a husband, noble and handsome," cried Lady Jane Dormer.

"He's well enough — with his elegant hat on, but when he takes it off — "

"Did you ever see such an odd head — "

"It's shaped like an egg!"

"But what a wrinkled brow!"

"And a snub nose."

"And watery eyes!"

"Heavy-lidded as though he were half-asleep."

"Did you ever see such straggly, sandy hair?"

The ladies' comments were interspersed with bursts of hilarious laughter, and the mother of the maids had much ado to quell their high spirits. All except Katherine, who crept into her truckle bed, taking no part in the gaiety. Though she had not lacked partners in the dancing, for her delicate beauty always attracted attention, her heart was not in it. She wondered if Lord Hertford was at that moment dancing with Lady Arabella Mewtas. Did he regret his declaration of love for Katherine, made impulsively before his mothcr? Why had he not gone straight to the Queen when they had returned to court, and asked for her consent to their match, as he had vowed he would do?

"What ails you, Kate?" asked Jane Dormer sympathetically.

"I'm weary of their nonsense, and shall be glad to return to the palace at Westminster."

"That may not be for some time yet," said Jane.

"Some time? But I thought we were setting off tomorrow."

"So we are. But only so far as Basing Hall, where their Majesties' honeymoon will begin."

"Alas! I thought we were for London."

"Why are you so dismayed? At Basing Hall the Marquis of Winchester will devise many amusements for their Majesties' pleasure. We shall be well entertained there. There will be balls and jousts and merriment of all kinds."

"A plague upon them all."

"For what — no, for whom do you wish to return to Westminster?"

"Nobody."

"Come now, confess."

"My — my little sister Mary will be lonely on her own."

"Fie, you know better than that. The Lady Mary will not be lonely."

"Why not?"

"I have seen her many times recently conversing most amiably with Master Keyes, and a more oddly assorted couple you never saw. He bends down to hear what she has to say, most courteously, from his six feet seven, to her three feet odd."

"Yes, it is true. I have seen them together. There is no harm in it. He is a very gentle man and he seems quite fond of my little sister."

Katherine had no desire for more probing as to her longing to return to London, so she pulled the coverlet over her head, signifying her desire for sleep, but sleep would not come. She tossed and turned, always the image before her of Lady Arabella Mewtas being borne away in Lord Hertford's arms, his face full of tender concern.

The following morning, as Lady Jane Dormer had foretold, a move was made to Basing Hall, where splendid entertainments were held, but to Lady Katherine's relief, within a week of the marriage, Queen Mary decided they should go to her castle at Windsor.

All Winchester turned out to see the royal party depart. Such comings and goings and tossings of plumed horses' heads and shrill orders from senoras and torrents of words from grandees, but at last all was ready, and Spanish cavaliers and their ladies together with English lords and ladies all embarked in fifty-two vividly painted coaches, each containing about twelve people, the royal bride and bridegroom in the scarlet coach. The whole cavalcade occasioned much astonishment among the country people, who ran to their doors to see it and to wave, as it lumbered through the villages.

At last Windsor Castle, and a crowd of ladies and gentlemen riding out to greet the royal couple. A waving of hats and salutations, the Queen all smiles and Prince Philip doffing his plumed cap and bowing. And behind them in one of the coaches, Lady Katherine was near to swooning with joy, for among the crowd of horsemen, she had caught sight of Lord Hertford, looking the most handsome and elegant of them all. He was anxiously looking from coach to coach, and Katherine waved to attract his attention. Lord Hertford saw her, doffed his cap, and edged his horse towards her coach.

"Kate," he cried, careless of who should overhear him, "here you are at last. How I've missed you!"

"Ned," she said, "Oh, Ned!" And all the misery, the jealousy and doubts were swept aside in a wave of delight. There was no opportunity then for more than those few words between them, but it was enough.

Entertainment on a lavish scale was held at Windsor. A grand festival of the Garter was held, in celebration of Philip's inauguration as its sovereign; the Spanish grandees were introduced to hunting the deer on a vast scale in Windsor Park; and in their turn the Spaniards gave a display of the contest known as "Jeugo des Cannes'. Don Philip and his cavaliers excelled at this and presented a colourful and exciting spectacle, mounted in various colours, Philip red, some in green, some in yellow, some in white, and some in blue. They bore targets and canes, and hurled the canes at each other's targets. Their trumpeters were dressed in their masters' colours and they had kettle drums and banners the colours of their garments.

Throughout these festivities, Ned and Katherine, though constantly seeing each other, were seldom able to be alone in each other's company.

At the end of August, the Queen decided to introduce her consort to the court at Westminster, and she and Philip, with all their suite, embarked on the Thames and were rowed in great pomp to Southwark. They crossed London Bridge on horseback, and were received with pageantry and outward rejoicing in the city. If the citizens of London were antagonistic towards Don Philip, their feelings were mollified by the sight of twenty carts which followed him, piled ostentatiously high with gold to fill their sovereign's treasury. The people took less kindly to the four or five hundred Spaniards belonging to the suites of the grandees attendant on Philip. They were soon to be the cause of perpetual trouble. Street fights between them and the English were of constant occurrence, and all sorts of brawls, as picturesque as they were bloody, between the English gentlemen and the Spanish cavaliers, and Spanish valets and London apprentices, occurred almost daily and especially at night.

The Queen was oblivious of this simmering discord and anxious only to reconcile the country to the see of Rome. To this end, Cardinal Pole was invited to England as an ambassador from the Pope. Parliament was alarmed, its members fearing they would lose the church property bestowed upon them by King Henry VIII. But when they were assured that they would not be required to part with their rich abbey lands, they were quite ready for reconciliation with Rome.

The year closed in an aura of contentment round the Queen. Her country was restored to the true faith, and she was happily married. Her benevolence was extended to her sister Elizabeth, who was pardoned, released from imprisonment, and joined the court for its Christmas festivities, which were of a very grand nature.

Never had the Lady Katherine looked prettier than on Christmas Eve when she entered the great hall of Westminster. Beneath the thousand lamps which lit the hall her red-gold curls glowed like the deep heart of a fire, and the gems in her dress winked and sparkled. Lord Hertford caught his breath as she glided towards him. Almost she seemed to be floating in a sea of light, in soft water of ever-changing hues. That the cunningly disposed lamps of various colours had the same flattering effect on all the ladies present was lost on Lord Hertford. He had eyes only for Kate, so much so that he brushed past the Princess Elizabeth without so much as a glance. This cavalier treatment astonished the tall and lovely princess, who expected all heads to turn at her approach.

Princess Elizabeth looked more than once during the course of the evening at her cousin Katherine, next in succession to the throne after herself. She noticed Lord Hertford, son of the Protector Somerset, who had died by the axe, partner Lady Katherine in the galliard; the Lady Katherine's father, too, had died by the axe, and her sister's aspirations to the throne had ended on the block. But Katherine and Ned Hertford had thoughts only for each other as they sat side by side and laughed inordinately at the droll fellows on hobbihorses who danced and capered for the amusement of the court; applauded the madrigals and joined in the jigs. Queen Mary, her husband at her side, presided benevolently over the festivities, happy in the expectation that soon there would be an heir to the throne.

The year ended, and the new year began in an atmosphere of optimism. Spring was in the air. Snowdrops bloomed in cottage gardens and in the hedgerows hazel wands hung out their golden tassels.

"The queen is pregnant," rumour said, and the rumour was not contradicted. An heir to the throne was expected. In

London, expansion was the word. The city would push its commerce to the uttermost ends of the earth and would grow rich and powerful. Beggars in the gutters raised their faces to the sun and felt its warmth through filthy rags upon their thin bodies.

Queen Mary retired to her palace at Richmond, and here a nursery was prepared. All was excitement and expectancy. No one looked forward more keenly to the birth than did the Lady Katherine and Lord Hertford.

"So soon as the Queen has an heir to the throne, I will beg her permission to marry you, sweet Kate."

"She cannot refuse you, Ned. There is no reason why we should not wed."

"You will be fourth in succession when the baby is born. You are still very close to the throne."

"But not for long. There will be many babies, one after another. You will see, Ned. And I shall be of no importance whatsoever to Queen Mary. She is well disposed towards us. There is no reason why she should refuse us."

"No. But we must wait a little longer.

Just until the baby is born."

But soon the heir to the throne was overdue. Would he or she never be born? Doubt was expressed, at first covertly, then openly. At last it became apparent that the Queen's indisposition was not occasioned by pregnancy, but her increased girth was due to dropsy. She was a prey to the severest headaches, her head being frightfully swelled; she was likewise subject to perpetual attacks of hysteria. Sometimes she lay weeks without speaking.

While the Queen lay torpid and half-dead, a horrible persecution of the Protestants began. King Philip said he would rather be without a kingdom than reign over heretics. And smoke from the fires at Smithfield where martyrs to the Protestant faith were burnt to death drifted over the city. In June war with France was proclaimed in London. King Philip left England to prosecute the war and Queen Mary never saw him again. In the autumn she was put into a litter and carried to London.

The Queen's ladies sat in Master Thomas Keyes' apartments, talking quietly as they worked at their tapestries. They no longer danced or played the lute. The news from France was bad. Calais, the last British possession was in jeopardy, and here at home the Queen was woefully ill.

Lady Mary Grey, dwarfish sister to Lady Katherine, offered wine and almond biscuits which all were too downcast to eat. For some time past this little lady, as much above Master Keyes socially, as she was beneath him in physical stature, had been accepted as hostess in his apartments. It was a strange alliance, Lady Mary being younger than this lofty widower's own children.

Lady Jane Dormer, the Queen's favourite lady-in-waiting, entered the apartment.

"How is her Grace?" she was asked.

"Desperately ill," was the reply, "and sunk in black despair. She has sat all day upon the floor, her hands clasping her knees, and her forehead resting upon them. Her hair streams about her, unkempt as a witches."

"Does she not eat or speak to you?"

"She will not eat, and once only has she spoken all the day. She raised her head to say that she would die, and if her breast were opened, Calais would be found written upon her heart.

"Poor lady!"

When Lady Jane Dormer was sent to Hatfield to take the Queen's jewels to her sister Elizabeth, it was understood that the Queen was dying and that Princess Elizabeth would succeed her.

Soon the whole court, on one pretext or another, found occasion to leave St James's Palace for Hatfield. Courtiers passed and re-passed on the road, while the Queen lay quietly in her bedchamber.

Between four and five o'clock one morning in November, after receiving extreme unction, at her desire Mass was celebrated in her chamber; at the elevation of the Host she raised her eyes to heaven, and at the benediction bowed her head and died.

8

HERALDS at the Palace of Westminster with solemn soundings of trumpets proclaimed 'Elizabeth, by the grace of God Queen of England, France and Ireland, and defender of the faith.' Proclamations were also made in the city at the cross of Cheapside, and London sprang to life. Its citizens forgot to mourn the death of Queen Mary in their joy for the accession of her sister. All the city bells rang, bonfires were lighted, ale and wine distributed and the populace invited to feast at tables put out at the doors of the rich citizens.

The court, ostensibly in mourning for Queen Mary, whose body lay at St James's Palace until her funeral, found it impossible not to share in this atmosphere of excited anticipation, as it prepared to receive her Majesty, Queen Elizabeth. She came in great state to her metropolis, a great retinue of lords and ladies escorting her to the

Tower of London.

Crowds thronged the streets to greet the Queen as she entered the city on horseback in a riding-dress of purple velvet with a scarf tied over her shoulder. At her side rode her favourite, Lord Robert Dudley. She was greeted by great volleys of gun-fire, by choruses of children and cheers from the excited crowds.

A very different procession set out a few days later from the palace of St James to escort the late Queen Mary to her last resting-place, with sombre pomp. Queen Elizabeth followed the hearse and behind her rode Lady Katherine, next in succession to the throne, with her sister, Lady Mary Grey. The little Lady Mary had difficulty in mounting the great black horse which she was expected to ride, encumbered as she was by a lengthy black train to her riding habit. Her good friend, Serjeant Keyes, saw her dilemma. He picked her up in his strong arms as though she were a baby and deposited her in the saddle.

Next came a long procession of monks, mourning for themselves as well as for their Queen, for none knew what his fate would be under the new Protestant queen.

That the Lady Katherine did not stand high in Queen Elizabeth's favour was soon evident. In spite of or perhaps because of, their nearness to the throne, she and her sister were relegated to Ladies of the Bedchamber instead of Ladies of the Privy Chamber. The Queen would brook no rivals. Elizabeth was young and tall and handsome, with glistening red hair, blue eyes and pale olive skin. With her easy carriage, quick wit and radiant vitality she became extremely popular wherever she went, and loved playing to the gallery, appearing in the most gorgeous and extravagant attire. Soon the one question on everybody's lips around her court, and indeed throughout the country was, "Whom will she marry?"

Her hand was sought by a dozen suitors at a time. They came and went; her brother-in-law, Philip of Spain, so lately widowed; Charles IX of France; the King of Sweden; a prince of Denmark; a Russian czar; dukes from every corner of the civilized world, and many aspirants from among her own court circle.

It was a great time for gambling and bets were laid for or against this or that suitor, and the date of the wedding. But always at the Queen's side was Lord Robert Dudley, brother to ill-fated Guildford Dudley. The Queen and Robert Dudley made a wonderful pair. Tall, dark and handsome, graceful and dashing, witty and accomplished, Robert Dudley had no peer. But Robert Dudley already had a wife. At the age of eighteen, carried away by a pretty face, he had married Amy Robsart, a little nobody. Had he been free, he would undoubtedly have been married off to Lady Jane Grey, instead of his younger brother, Guildford. So, if his ill-considered marriage was keeping him from the throne, it had also saved him from the block.

That the Queen was deeply in love with Robert Dudley was evident, but it did not prevent her from entertaining those who came to woo her, and listening attentively to what they had to say. Underneath her apparent frivolity, she was shrewd and prudent; careful not to upset one side or the other. Her sister Mary had loved God and sought to serve

Him by imposing her own faith upon the whole country. Elizabeth loved her countrymen and in the matter of religion sought a compromise which would be acceptable to all. In this as in all affairs of state she was wise. Even her unruly heart was controlled by her cool head. She gathered round her as her advisers, men of vision and shrewd insight. With their help Elizabeth put the country's finances on a sound footing, calmed the violence of conflicting religious opinions, and kept those foreign powers, France and Spain, firmly in their places.

Lord Robert Dudley, the Queen made Master of her horse, an office which he graced to perfection and which kept him by her side. Tongues wagged constantly about these two, and conflicting reports were put about regarding Amy Robsart, who was living in seclusion, neglected by her husband, at Cumnor Hall, near Oxford.

On St George's Day, the Lord Robert Dudley was elected a Knight of the Garter, and after the ceremony there was an aquatic festival in honour of the Queen. The Lady Katherine and others of the court who were not required in attendance, took up positions at Master Keyes' windows to enjoy the pageant. The river was crammed with boats and barges, and thousands of people thronged its banks, determined to see the Queen and to enjoy the spectacle. As she was rowed up and down, Robert Dudley by her side, trumpets blew, drums beat, flutes played, guns were discharged and fireworks exploded.

It was ten o'clock at night before the Queen departed, but the courtiers crowded round Master Keyes' windows watched until the last boat had gone, the last flare extinguished, and the river deserted, its water gleaming palely from the light of the moon. They had all been sitting in the dark, the better to enjoy the spectacle on the river, Katherine very close to Ned, their hands interlocked.

Among the company was Blanche Parry, the Queen's confidential maid, a renowned fortune-teller and reader of palms. When the candles were lit, Lady Katherine said to her. "When shall Ned and I be wed? Do my hand for me, Blanche."

Blanche Parry took her hands by the wrists and studied them carefully.

"Well? What do you see in my hands? What do the lines say?" demanded Katherine impatiently.

Blanche Parry seemed reluctant to speak, but upon being pressed further answered, "The lines say, madam, that if you ever marry without the Queen's consent in writing, you and your husband will be undone, and your fate worse than that of your sister, Lady Jane."

"You are making it all up," said Katherine, snatching her hands away.

"Don't worry, sweetheart. We'll get the Queen's consent at once," consoled Hertford. "I will beg an audience of her tomorrow."

But the Queen had other matters to attend to, and Hertford could not get an audience with her. Perhaps he did not try very hard. They were all a little afraid of Queen Elizabeth. For all her generous disposition, her gaiety and her tolerance, she was apt upon occasion to fly into uncontrollable rages, and Hertford may have judged discretion to be the better part of valour.

So the affair of Lady Katherine and Lord Hertford, though well-known and discussed freely by their intimate friends in the privacy of Serjeant Keyes' apartments, was kept a secret from the Queen.

Life at court became a series of pageants and progresses, very different from the sober atmosphere of the late Queen Mary, whose household had been almost monastic. What with Mass every morning, saying the rosary, evening and night prayers and pious readings in between, there had been precious little time for levity, except for that brief idyllic spell when Mary and Philip of Spain were first married.

There had been religious processions, but nothing to compare with Elizabeth's devotions, which were often conducted in such a manner as to afford an excuse for a public holiday.

At the end of Lent, the entire court went in great state, to hear a sermon delivered from the cross at St Mary's, Spital. Queen Elizabeth wore a farthingale four yards in circumference, and an enormous cartwheel of a ruff which made her head appcar to be in the centre of her body. She was attended by one thousand men in harness, in shirts of mail, bearing pikes, with drums and trumpets sounding. The procession was closed by morris dancers. Two white bears in a cart brought up the rear, and remained in waiting during the preaching. At the conclusion of the sermon, courtiers and citizens alike were entertained by morris dancing and bear baiting.

The following Thursday the court adjourned to Greenwich for the Maundy Service, which took place with great pomp and pageantry. Lady Katherine and Lady Mary, together with all the Queen's maids of honour and gentlewomen took part. The palace hall was prepared with a long table on each side, with benches, carpets and cushions, and a cross table at the upper end where the Queen's chaplain stood. Thirty-two poor women, being the same number as the years of her Majesty's age at that time, dressed in their best and all looking very neat, except that their feet were bare were ushered in and seated on the forms, where they waited, looking a little shy and ill-at-ease; then the yeoman of the laundry came with a fair towel and a silver basin filled with warm water and sweet flowers and washed all their feet, one after the other; he likewise made a cross a little above the toes, and kissed each foot after drying. The sub-almoner performed the same ceremony, and the Queen's almoner also.

Then her Majesty entered the hall, and went to a prie-dieu and cushion, placed in the space between the two tables, and remained during prayers and singing, and while the gospel was read telling how Christ washed His apostles' feet. Then it was the turn of the Queen's maids of honour and gentlewomen, armed with aprons and towels, each carrying a silver basin with warm water, spring flowers and sweet herbs. Her Majesty, kneeling on the cushion placed for the purpose, proceeded to wash, in turn, one of the feet of each of the poor women, and wiped them, with the assistance of the basin-bearers; moreover she crossed and kissed them, as the others had done.

The feet of the poor women had never been so washed, they were almost washed away, especially as it was evident by their spotless state before the ceremonies were begun that each pair of feet had been subjected to a good scrubbing before they ever entered the Queen's palace.

The ceremony was not yet over, for the Queen now gave each woman sufficient broad cloth for a gown and a pair of shoes, a wooden platter, whereon was half a side of salmon, as much ling, six red herrings, two manchets, and a mazer or wooden cup, full of claret. All these things she gave separately. Then her gentlewomen each delivered to her Majesty the towel and apron used in the ablutions, and she gave each of the poor women one a-piece. The treasurer of the royal chamber then brought the Queen thirty-two small white purses, made of wash-leather, with very long strings each with thirty-two pence within, one for each poor woman. The treasurer then supplied her with thirty-two red purses, each containing twenty shillings. This she distributed to redeem the gown she wore, which by ancient custom had been given to one chosen among the number.

Well pleased with herself the Queen now took her ease on her cushion of state and listened awhile to the choir, the women remaining in her presence until she retired, near sunset.

This elaborate ceremony, though somewhat far removed from the simple act of service and humility performed by Christ to His apostles, gave great pleasure to the fortunate recipients of the Maundy, and induced in her Majesty a state of complacent benevolence.

Lady Katherine and her sister were suddenly called away from these diversions by their mother, who had given birth to a child, a little girl, who had died almost at once. Lady Suffolk had been exceedingly ill and it was thought that she would die as well.

The Queen was pleased to lend Lady Katherine and Lady Mary her own palanquin, in which they arrived at Sheen, where their mother was living, one windy day in March, escorted by Lord Hertford. Lady Suffolk was very pleased to see them all. She had regained some of her strength and propped up by pillows she listened sympathetically to Lord Hertford when he asked her for Lady Katherine's hand in marriage.

Lady Suffolk took Hertford's hand in hers affectionately and said, "You would make a very suitable husband for my daughter Katherine if the Queen would only see it in the same light, but I will have nothing to do with the matter unless with the Queen's knowledge and consent, and also that of her council."

She took Lady Katherine's hand in her own free hand and said, "Daughter Kate, I have found you a husband."

Katherine bent her head to hide the smile which she could not suppress and said meekly, "I am very willing to love Ned."

To have her mother sympathetic to them was something gained, but the necessity to tell the Queen and gain her consent remained just as much of an obstacle.

"I will appeal to the Queen on your behalf" Lady Suffolk said. "Adrian, frame a letter for me."

Adrian Stokes bent over his wife and settled her more comfortably on her pillows. "I will do so gladly," he said.

Adrian Stokes had been secretary to Lady Suffolk as well as groom before their marriage, and she depended upon him entirely now.

While Lady Katherine and little Lady Mary chatted to their mother and described the Queen's latest extravaganza, Hertford and Adrian Stokes together composed a letter for her to the Queen, humbly requesting that she would be pleased to assent to the marriage of Lady Katherine to Lord Hertford. It was, they wrote, "the only thing she desired before her death and should be the occasion for her to die the more quietly."

Lady Suffolk was satisfied with the wording of the letter and took the pen into her hand and signed it. She gave it to Hertford and told him to deliver it to the Queen at once. They then returned to London.

Lord Hertford was thoughtful and uneasy throughout the return journey and obviously was not looking forward to his task of delivering the letter.

"The Queen will fly into a terrible rage when she reads this letter. The last thing she desires is for you to marry and beget an heir to the throne."

"Then why does she not marry herself

and put an end to all this dilly-dallying?" asked Katherine, impatiently.

"You know full well the reason. It is her love for Lord Robert Dudley that keeps her single."

"But she cannot expect me to remain unwed for ever!"

"We must wait a little longer. It would be very unwise to anger the Queen."

"So you will not deliver my mother's letter?"

"We must wait," said Hertford, uneasily.

"Wait, wait, wait! We do nothing but wait. If you will not give my mother's letter to the Queen, I will do it myself. Give it to me."

"No, no. We must not give the letter to the Queen. Not yet."

Katherine's face went very white. "You are afraid to approach her Majesty."

Hertford flared into sudden anger, stung by the truth of this statement.

"I do not care to meddle any more in the matter," he said flatly.

"Very well," replied Katherine, "there is no more to be said. All is over between us, and I wish you farewell."

They parted without another word,

both hurt and angry, bewildered, too, to feel such sudden bitterness take the place of tender love.

The gaiety of the court increased in tempo in a period of peace and plenty and Queen Elizabeth was very popular. People flocked to the river Thames to catch a glimpse of her whenever she took her pleasure in her state barge. A fine new ship was launched at Woolwich, which in honour of the Queen was called the 'Elizabeth'.

In July of that year the whole court withdrew to her bower at Greenwich to be entertained to a series of tournaments and masques. The pageantry was shared alike by the court and the citizens of London, who poured out of the town to participate in the festivities at Greenwich.

Queen Elizabeth rode to Greenwich on a pillion behind Lord Robert Dudley, and the people not only greeted her, as was their wont, when she appeared among them, with rapturous acclamations, but in their eagerness to get near her, to catch a look, a word, or perhaps to snatch a jewelled button or aglet from her dress, thronged her Majesty almost to suffocation. Her noble equerry, then as a matter of necessity, used his riding-whip very smartly, to drive the boldest of them back; whereupon her Majesty graciously interposed ever and anon, crying, "Prithee my lord, take heed that thou hurt not my loving people. Pray, my lord, do not hurt any of my loving people." But when, in obedience to these tender remonstrances, he desisted, and she found herself incommoded by the pressure of the crowd and her progress impeded, she said to the earl, in a low voice, "Cut them again, my lord. Cut them again."

A goodly banqueting-house of fir poles was built up in one of the glades of the park to refresh the court at a royal and military *fête champêtre*. The pavilion was decked with birch branches, and all manner of flowers, roses, lavender and marigolds. Sweet herbs were strewn with the rushes. A great space was made for a muster of fourteen hundred men-at-arms clad in velvet and chains of gold, with guns, morris-pikes, halberds and flags. When it had been reviewed a mock battle was staged, with flourish of trumpets, alarm of drums, and melody of flutes. Three onsets were given to great applause. Afterwards there was a running at tilt, then all the people danced.

Lads and lasses, gay in summer finery, strolled about hand-in-hand and kissed beneath the trees. Children darted about like fireflies, and sober matrons gossiped together in the sunshine, while their husbands quaffed beer and flirted with the wenches in the refreshment tents.

In this relaxed and happy atmosphere court etiquette was lessened and there were as many flirtations among the courtiers as the commoners. Ned Hertford was seen sitting at the feet of Sir Peter Mewtas's pretty daughter, Arabella, and Katherine, her head high, though her heart was breaking, strolled through the glades in the gathering dusk with that feeble boy Herbert, son of Lord Pembroke, to whom she had once been married. Oh, it was a night for strolling hand-in-hand, and they were followed by Feria, the Spanish ambassador, and Lady Jane Dormer.

The festivities ended with a firework display and the firing of guns at midnight and gradually the crowds dispersed, reluctant to exchange Greenwich's balmy air, for the stifling atmosphere of London town. Lady Katherine walked alone towards Greenwich Palace, beneath a star-lit sky.

"My lady," called a voice behind her, "wait for us. We have tidings for you."

She turned and saw Don Feria walking arm-in-arm with her friend, Jane Dormer. One glance at their faces conveyed the news they wished her to know.

"My dearest Jane," she said, "I am so happy for you," and she embraced her friend and kissed her, then shaking hands with Don Feria, said, "I congratulate you, sir, with all my heart."

"But you, Katherine," cried Lady Jane, "Why do you walk alone? We saw you not long since, with Lord Herbert Pembroke."

"Oh him!" cried Katherine contemptuously, "I sent him about his business."

"How did he displease you?"

"He had the effrontery to suggest that we should be wedded again. I asked him whether he had fallen in love with me, and he answered no, but it was his father's will that we should remarry."

"Remarry Lord Herbert Pembroke! But why?" asked Jane Dormer.

"Once, if you remember, for a brief spell, his father, Lord Pembroke was father-in-law to the Queen's sister," answered Lady Katherine bitterly. "Now his ambition is to be grandsire of the King of England, for I am next in succession to the throne. The Queen has no eyes for anybody but Dudley, in spite of all the claimants for her hand, and him she cannot marry for he already has a wife."

"She will surely marry somebody else and get herself an heir to the throne."

"Perhaps," agreed Lady Katherine, "if only to keep me from it. She cannot bear to think of me or mine as her possible successor, and I experience nothing but discourtesy from her Grace."

"You are unhappy at the court of Queen Elizabeth?" enquired the Count de Feria.

"I am unhappy," agreed Katherine. "Queen Mary always treated me with great kindness, but not so her sister. Queen Elizabeth has put me and my sister down from our positions in the Privy Chamber to the Bedchamber. She bears us no good-will."

The Count de Feria listened to Lady Katherine with great interest.

"Do not marry," he said abruptly, "without consulting me."

Lady Katherine was startled. She was aware of being appraised by this Spanish statesman. But she agreed with him politely, then bade them both good-night.

In spite of the lateness of the hour, the Count de Feria went to his desk to give his master King Phillip II of Spain a full account of the situation at the English court; of the Queen's passion for Robert Dudley who already had a wife; of her dislike for Lady Katherine Grey, who was heir apparent to the English throne; of the beauty, sweetness and docility of Lady Katherine and of the suitability of marrying her off to Philip's son, the imbecile Don Carlos.

Katherine tossed and turned in her bed, sleepless, ignorant of the political web which was being spun round her, indifferent to the possibility of becoming

Queen of England, but suffering agonies of jealousy and humiliation at Ned's obvious preference for Arabella Mewtas to herself.

Queen Elizabeth, escorted everywhere by Robert Dudley, was the centre and inspiration of lighthearted gaiety, of *fêtes champêtres*, tournaments, masques and tourneys for the rest of that brilliant summer. As the fun waxed faster, her popularity increased.

Lady Katherine, and her sister Lady Mary, took little part in these festivities, for their mother, the Duchess of Suffolk became desperately ill, and with the Queen's permission, they went often to visit her. Her fondness for Adrian Stokes had softened her, and during her last year she had grown more gentle and kind. She was genuinely concerned with procuring the Queen's consent to Katherine's marriage with Lord Hertford, and, ignorant of the rift between them, with her dying breath repeated the last words of her ill-fated letter to the Queen.

"Tell her Majesty," Lady Frances whispered, "the marriage of my daughter to Lord Hertford, my dearest son, is the only thing I desire before I die, and will be the occasion for me to die more quietly."

Lady Suffolk had never showered a great abundance of affection on her daughters, nevertheless she was their only close relative except for Lord John Grey, their uncle, who lived mostly at Havering in Essex and seldom saw them. They returned forlornly to Westminster, to the Queen who only tolerated their presence, and reported their mother's death. Surprisingly, she treated them with great kindness and insisted that her cousin, the Duchess of Suffolk be buried with royal honours. As befitted princesses of the blood royal, Lady Katherine and Lady Mary knelt on cushions before the altar, their mourning trains held by Ladies of the Bedchamber.

Now, in her softened mood towards Lady Katherine, was the moment to give the Queen Lady Suffolk's last message.

"Tell her Majesty the marriage of my daughter to Lord Hertford, my dearest son, is the only thing I desire before I die."

But since Lord Hertford patently no longer desired this marriage, there was no object in gaining the Queen's permission, and the moment passed. The two sisters accepted their stepfather's invitation to return with him to Sheen immediately after the funeral, and they all travelled back together in the chariot which had borne the coffin to the Abbey. Everything had been left to Adrian Stokes. He was kind to his stepdaughters and anxious for them to make their home with him, and for a time they remained. But Lady Katherine was restless and wished only to return to court, so after a little while they left him and went back to London.

Lady Jane Seymour was delighted with the return of Lady Katherine. "Come to my chamber," she insisted, "and we can talk together without interruption."

Lady Katherine was only too pleased to do so, but once comfortably installed with her friend there soon fell a silence between them. Katherine longed only to ask after Ned, and his sister desired to speak of him, but both were shy of broaching the subject. Their silence was broken by the entrance of Lord Hertford himself.

"Sister," he began, "I have come to ask — " The words died away on his lips as he saw Katherine. They stared at each other, the colour mounting in Katherine's cheeks, then Ned Hertford took a step towards her, his hands outstretched.

"Kate," he said, "sweet Kate," and they were in each other's arms.

Quietly, Lady Jane Seymour left the apartment, leaving the lovers alone together.

"Oh, my love, my dear love, I have missed you," cried Ned.

"And I you," said Katherine. "I have been so very unhappy."

"Your mother — I am sorry about her death."

"She died with your name on her lips," said Katherine. "Her 'dearest son' she called you, and her one desire was to see us wed. 'Tell the queen' she said, 'the marriage of my daughter to Lord Hertford, my dearest son, is the only thing I desire before I die, and will be the occasion for me to die more quietly'."

"Poor lady," said Ned.

"Our marriage is the only thing which *I* desire," cried Katherine.

"And I also," agreed Hertford.

"But her Majesty will never agree to it. Although she has been kind lately, she has no real liking for me, and would heartily dislike to see a son of mine ascend the throne."

"If only she would wed, and beget herself a son and heir she would have no cause to complain of our marriage."

"Perhaps she will, soon. It seems the court is as full as ever of suitors for her hand."

"Aye, they come and go from every corner of the earth and the Queen entertains them all. Prince John of Sweden is the latest one. Her Majesty sent us all in our richest array to receive him at Leadenhall with an escort of one hundred yeomen on horseback, all blowing trumpets!"

"And all the townsfolk on holiday to see the procession, I doubt not," said Katherine.

"Aye, the streets were full, and the Swedish prince threw handfuls of silver as he passed by. Such scrambling and cheers and shouting as never was seen. It's a wonder nobody was trampled to death."

"And what are Prince John's chances of marrying the Queen?"

"No better than her other suitors, I fear, though a tournament was lately held at court in his honour. He sat next to the queen in the gallery where they looked down on milords Robert Dudley and Hunsdon, who held four courses against all comers. Eighteen opponents, well armed and appointed appeared and broke lances against the maintenants, and all parties acquitted themselves very well, but it was obvious to us all who looked on, that the Queen had no eyes for anybody but the gallant Lord Robert."

"We must just wait until her Grace makes up her mind. She surely cannot mean to remain single for ever. But, in the meantime, do not stop loving me, dear Ned."

"Never fear. I shall love you with all my heart, until death parts us, but marry you I will, and that soon."

They parted reluctantly, both delighted that love was renewed between them.

The Queen was well content for the handsome Swedish prince to remain at court and amuse her with his flattery and attention, and he remained over Christmas and into the New Year. On New Year's Day he went to court gorgeously apparelled, with an equestrian retinue decked out in velvet jerkins and rich gold chains. Not to be outdone, Queen Elizabeth appeared in a vast ruff and vaster farthingale and a bushel of pearls. Her hair was loaded with crowns and powdered with diamonds.

A great variety of pleasure had been devised in honour of Prince John. First there was bear-baiting, then a company of Morris men begged leave to dance before her Majesty, and the antics of some hobbihorses and players masked like giraffes and lions pleased her mightily. Elizabeth sat in her gallery, Prince John on her right and Lord Robert Dudley on her left, but when she descended to the hall to lead the galiarde, it was Robert Dudley who partnered her, not Prince John. The Queen danced with great spirit, raising her petticoats to reveal the knitted black silk stockings which had been her silk-woman's present to her that very day. They pleased her so much that she declared she would never more wear cloth stockings.

Queen Elizabeth returned to her seat, laughing and breathless and the players begged leave to perform a jig, a play with dancing. It began with a sprightly matron skipping for joy at the departure of her husband on a journey. She was soon joined by her paramour, and together with her servants they performed an intricate measure. It was evident that this was meant to depict a house of some wealth and it was soon plain that the lady's lover was also her groom.

There were smothered titters from some of the younger courtiers and a voice was heard to say, "'Tis all the fashion to be seduced by one's horse-keeper." It was the Lady Katherine who spoke so rashly and all heads were turned in her direction. Perhaps she did not realize that she spoke so loud, or else there was a lull in the proceedings; at all events this unfortunate remark was clearly heard by the assembled company, including the Queen. She was very angry;

so angry that she took off her slipper and hurled it at the actors, declaring that she would look no more at such nonsense.

The court was thrown into consternation and the poor players were completely bewildered, having no idea how they had offended their fair young Queen, for they were ignorant of court gossip, and did not know of the favours which her Majesty had bestowed upon her master of the horse. However, some tumblers were hastily substituted for the actors in the jig, and presently some madrigals were sung so sweetly that the Queen's equilibrium was restored. Nevertheless, heads were shaken over the Lady Katherine's indiscretion. She, above all people, needed to be in the Queen's favour.

The Duc de Feria seated himself beside the Lady Katherine.

"You are out of favour, madam," he observed.

"It is no new thing for me," flamed Katherine, who wished with all her heart she had never made so stupid a remark.

"How would you like to exchange this court for another?" asked Feria.

"What do you mean, sir?"

"I cannot speak frankly to you here, lest we are overheard. Will you meet me in Master Keyes' apartments tomorrow forenoon?"

"Willingly," agreed Katherine, lightly, but in her heart she felt dismayed.

She remembered the Duc de Feria's conversation with her at Greenwich after the fireworks, and she reminded herself that he was the Spanish ambassador. Could it be that she was singled out to be the bride of Don Carlos? Oh, no! Not that imbecile son of King Philip. She must tell Feria at once that she would marry none other than Lord Hertford. But how could she tell him? She trembled to think of the Queen hearing of this in a roundabout fashion. Too many people knew already. There was only one thing to be done. Ned *must* approach her Majesty at once and beg permission for the match. But no, it would never be given, especially as she had now angered the Queen.

With such reflections, Katherine tortured herself until the time came to meet Don Feria. He was already waiting in Thomas

Keyes' apartment, idly passing the time of day with Blanche Parry, Queen Elizabeth's favourite woman. Blanche Parry excused herself and left the two together.

Don Feria began by commiserating with Lady Katherine on her mother's recent death, leaving her and her sister orphaned and impecunious. He was about to enlarge on the advantages that would be hers if she would agree to an alliance with Don Carlos of Spain, when, to the astonishment of them both the Queen herself swept into the apartment, followed by Blanche Parry. They rose hastily, the Duc de Feria bowing low and Lady Katherine curtseying, but the Queen graciously begged them to continue their conversation.

"I am come to inspect my Serjeant-porter's rooms," she observed. "I understand much merriment goes on among my maids in Master Keyes' apartments."

She walked to the windows and gazed down to the wide water of the Thames, continuing, "Ah yes, there is a pleasant outlook from these windows. Go, Blanche, and find us some refreshment."

Thomas Keyes arrived, and handed malmsey and sweet cakes to her Majesty, greatly flattered by her patronage, and never had the Queen been more gracious to all around her.

The Duc de Feria's moment for confidential talk with Lady Katherine was lost. Indeed, the Queen now seemed bent on having Lady Katherine by her side at all times, often referred to her as her 'dearest sister' and restored her and the little Lady Mary to their former positions as Ladies of the Privy Chamber. This was a matter of some bewilderment to Lady Katherine, who could not know of the correspondence which was passing secretly between the English ambassador at the court of King Philip of Spain, and the Queen's secretary, Lord Cecil. But Queen Elizabeth was well aware of the Spanish plot to marry off the Lady Katherine to Don Carlos, to balance the potential power of France, whose young Dauphin had just married the Queen of Scotland, who also had claims to the English throne.

So the Lady Katherine must now be

kept by the Queen's side at all costs, and must accompany her Majesty on her royal progress in the spring.

The freshness of the countryside was lost on Lady Katherine as they travelled into the depths of Essex. Her heart's desire was further from her than ever. Either she was to be kept a spinster by the Queen's will, or she was to be snatched from her Majesty's side to be married to a Spanish imbecile. And in the meantime, while the Queen tarried at Ingatestone, enjoying lavish entertainment at the expense of Sir William Petre, no doubt Lord Hertford was consoling himself with the company of that minx, Lady Arabella Mewtas.

At last the progress was over and Lady Katherine once more pouring out her doubts and fears to her friend and confidant, Lady Jane Seymour.

"He cares only for you, I know. He has told me many times he will marry you at once, so soon as he can get permission from the Queen."

"We shall never get permission from the Queen. It grows more and more impossible to ask her."

"When her Majesty has a child to succeed her, your problems will be resolved."

"A child! Yes, but first she must get herself a husband, and that seems as far off as ever with Robert Dudley so constantly by her side."

"Have patience, and in the meantime you and my brother shall meet whenever possible here in my room. I will arrange it for you, and there will be no fear of discovery."

Katherine sighed, then smiled at Jane Seymour wanly. "You are my good friend," she said. "Whatever should I do without you to confide in?"

"There are strange rumours circulating round Amy Dudley," said Jane Seymour.

"What sort of rumours?"

"She is living in seclusion as you know at Cumnor, near Oxford. She has been gravely ill and in deep depression."

"Poor woman," said Katherine. "What is her complaint, apart, I mean, from having her husband filched from her by the Queen?"

"Some say that she is suffering from cancer of the breast, and is in great pain from it. Others say — " Lady Jane hesitated.

"What do others say?"

"That she is being poisoned," said Jane Seymour in a whisper.

"Poisoned? Not by — ?"

"By his orders, so it is said."

"Do you think it is true?"

"I do not know."

Katherine pondered this strange gossip in horrified silence. She was appalled to find herself wishing it were true. If only the Queen were able to marry Lord Robert Dudley and to beget heirs to the throne, surely there could be no objection to her own marriage to Hertford, and no more plots to marry her off to some foreign prince.

Summer succeeded spring, with Lady Katherine and Lord Hertford meeting alone occasionally by stealth in his sister's chamber and often in the company of others in Thomas Keyes' rooms.

On a bright afternoon in early autumn, Lady Katherine and Lord Hertford with several other young courtiers were amusing themselves with music and gossip when Blanche Parry entered and said dramatically, "The Lady Dudley is dead!"

There was a shocked silence until somebody asked, "How?"

"She fell downstairs and broke her neck," said Blanche. "My lord Robert Dudley has ridden off post haste to Oxford to attend her inquest."

A babble of chatter broke out. Rumour, gossip and scraps of secret information were bandied about. The dam of silence was breached. Everybody had something scandalous to tell of the relationship between the Queen and Robert Dudley, and all were ready to believe that this brilliant courtier, this favourite of the Queen, had engineered his own wife's death.

The whole court was buzzing with stories of Elizabeth and Robert Dudley; how he had on more than one occasion usurped the duties of the ladies of the bedchamber in assisting the Queen at her toilet; that he had been seen handing to her Majesty garments which ought never to have been seen in the hands of her master of horse! How on her numerous progressions she always insisted on Robert Dudley's chamber being adjacent to her own.

In a few days Lord Robert Dudley returned to court. The inquest had been held and a verdict of accidental death was given. Few people believed it. Some said it was suicide, others murder. On the morning of Lady Dudley's death she had given permission for all her household to go to the fair being held in the nearby town of Abingdon, leaving her quite alone in the house. Upon their return she was found lying dead on the flagstones at the bottom of a flight of backstairs. Her maid, who loved her dearly, said that her mistress had been in a state of deep distress for some time and had often been seen on her knees praying to God to save her from despair. Whether her despair was on account of her illness, or of her husband's neglect of her was not clear, but many heads were shaken over the coroner's verdict of accidental death, and Lord Robert Dudley was much infamed.

But the Queen kept him by her side and showered favours on him, all but the ultimate favour of her hand in marriage and the shared throne of England. This the Queen withheld, although wild rumours circulated round the court to the effect that Robert Dudley was secretly married to the Queen in the presence of his brother and two ladies of the chamber.

9

FOR Lady Katherine to absent herself from court for as little as a day required express permission from her Majesty, but the Queen did allow her to spend a day with some friends at Bisham Abbey, Sir Thomas Hoby's place. Hertford contrived to be among the company and he and Katherine wandered hand-in-hand about the extensive grounds, oblivious of all except their desire to be together.

"My love, my little love," said Hertford, "you must wed me. I will not wait any longer. I *must* approach the Queen."

"It would be no good. She will never give her consent for you or anybody else to marry me. I am surprised that she allowed me out of her sight today. I am kept constantly by her side. It is not her fondness for me, you may be sure, but her fear that I shall be courted and wed. Even my little sister, Mary, is kept under her surveillance, but there is little fear that she will be desired."

"There you are wrong," said Hertford. "The little Lady Mary is greatly loved by that mountain of a man, Sergeant Keyes."

They both laughed, for it was indeed a ludicrous attachment, between Lady Mary and Sergeant Keyes, he so large and she so small.

"My grandmother, Princess Mary, was in as desperate a plight as we are," mused Katherine. "Her one desire was to marry grandfather, but her brother, King Henry VIII, insisted that she should marry old King Louis XII of France. She was only sixteen and he was over sixty."

"Poor child," said Hertford, "but did he not die soon after their marriage?"

"Just three months after, and while grandmother, now Queen Mary of France, was shut up, dressed in white, according to French tradition, for forty days of mourning, grandfather, the Duke of Suffolk, was sent by the King to escort her home to England. Grandmother was overjoyed to see him and, defying French custom, she secretly married him in the private chapel at the Hotel de

Cluny before her days of mourning were ended. When they returned to England and announced their marriage, the King was furious at first, but it was a *fait accompli* and he had to accept it."

"A *fait accompli*," said Ned. "We must follow your grandmother's example and present our monarch with a *fait accompli*. That is our only course."

"Oh, Ned," said Katherine, "dare we?"

They walked in silence, turning over the possibility of marrying in secret. The idea, once mooted, would not be dismissed, and they rode back to London in a state of suppressed excitement.

But Lord Hertford was taken ill with a fever and tossed and turned upon his bed in his house at Cannon Row, by the Thames, while Queen Elizabeth with her customary impetuosity swept her court off to Greenwich to enjoy a few days' hunting.

Lady Katherine's hopes were once more dashed, and her mood of buoyant excitement died. But Lord Hertford, on his bed of sickness, made up his mind that nothing would deter him, and the moment she returned to Westminster they would be betrothed.

He sent a message through his sister, and overjoyed, Katherine arranged to meet him in Jane's apartment. The meeting was of a formal nature, for although the wedding was to take place in secrecy, Lord Hertford was anxious that there should be no doubt about the legitimacy of their children. It was possible, after all, that he would father a sovereign of England.

With his sister Jane as witness, Lord Hertford, pale and wan from his illness said solemnly, "I have borne you goodwill for a long time, and because you should not think I intend to mock you, I am content, if you will, to marry you."

Lady Katherine replied demurely, "I like both you and your offer and am content to marry with you."

"When?" demanded Lord Hertford.

And Lady Katherine replied firmly, "Next time the Queen's Majesty shall leave the palace."

Then, his sister looking on, Ned took Katherine's hands in his, kissed her and put a ring upon her finger. Now they were formally betrothed and all three of them put their heads together to devise some place and means of performing the wedding ceremony. At last Lord Hertford went on his way leaving the two ladies together.

Katherine spread her fingers, displaying the ring to her friend. It was very handsome, with a fine pointed diamond, and was one which Lady Jane had often seen on her brother's own hand. Katherine was in an ecstasy of delight, "My little, my little love," she crooned, pressing the ring to her lips. "I am well pleased with thee."

"But you must not wear it. You must take it off at once," begged Lady Jane.

Reluctantly, Katherine took the ring from her finger.

"I will put it on a ribbon," she said, "and wear it always, secretly, next to my heart."

The time was between All-hallowtide and Christmas, and it was fine and bright though cold, just the right sort of weather to please the amazonian Queen

Elizabeth, and nobody was surprised to hear her say, "Tomorrow we will go to Eltham to hunt."

Lady Katherine and Lady Jane Seymour exchanged quick glances and the moment she was able to do so, Jane withdrew from the Queen's presence. She hastily wrote two letters, and instructed her man-servant to deliver one to Lord Hertford at his place in Cannon Row, and the other to a priest.

The next day promised well, and very early in the morning servants were hurrying about in a great froth of activity; immaculately groomed horses were champing in the courtyard, and tossing their plumed heads, and the Queen was in boisterous good spirits. Only Lady Katherine and Lady Jane appeared to be downcast and Lady Katherine's head was swathed in a great shawl.

"What ails you?" asked the Queen.

Lady Katherine mumbled something from the folds of her shawl, and Lady Jane interposed, "She is nearly demented with faceache, your Grace."

"Then let her return to her couch,"

the Queen answered impatiently. "She cannot hunt with her head so trussed."

"Shall I stay behind with her?" asked Lady Jane.

"Yes, yes, if you like," said the Queen, and swept away.

From a window inside the palace Katherine and Jane watched the brilliant cavalcade move off then Katherine snatched the shawl from her head, and stopping only to stuff into the pocket of her dress a three-cornered kerchief she and Jane donned cloaks and hoods and stealthily left the palace.

At his house in Cannon Row, Lord Hertford had risen at six o'clock and now waited in an agony of suspense for Katherine and Jane to arrive. He gave permission for his gentlemen-ushers, body-servants and groom to have the day off and desired them not to return until late afternoon. His man, Christopher Barnaby, he did not quite trust, so he told him to go to a goldsmith's in Fleet Street, with a letter of great importance.

"On no account return without an answer," said Lord Hertford, knowing full well that thc goldsmith would be away from the city until the wedding was all over.

These orders to Hertford's personal attendants caused considerable chatter in the kitchen, especially when commands were received to place bread, meat and comfits, with wine and ale, in my Lord Hertford's bedroom, and then for all the servants to remain below stairs until after their dinner, which they took at eleven o'clock.

Having prepared the food as instructed, the cook stationed himself discreetly at a window overlooking the watergate. At another window commanding a good view of the river, Barnaby watched, having decided that the letter to the goldsmith could wait a little while.

Lord Hertford paced about his rooms anxiously. All was in order, his bed made, his sideboard heaped with refreshments.

Unattended, Lady Katherine and Lady Jane hurried along the river bank, the tide being low. As they drew near to the watergate of Hertford's house, a cloaked figure passed them and would have slipped by but Lady Jane cried sharply, her nerves tense, "Whither go you, Barnaby?"

"On business of my lord's," he replied smoothly, and went on his way.

Lord Hertford himself now appeared at the watergate and escorted his visitors upstairs. Lady Katherine was breathless and agitated. She sank into a chair and tried to compose herself.

"Where is the priest?" enquired Hertford's sister.

"Not yet arrived," he answered.

They waited impatiently, nerves on edge, but no priest came.

"I will find another one," said Lady Jane resolutely. "There is no time to waste," and she left the house by herself.

Hertford tried to comfort Katherine but he was almost as agitated as she was. The priest's non-arrival looked like completely ruining their plans.

"Do not fret, my sweet," said Hertford. "My sister will find a cleric."

And before half-an-hour had elapsed, Lady Jane returned, followed by a priest, a stockily-built man with a red beard, dressed in a furred, black gown. She wanted no time in explanation, or introduction, so anxious was she to get the marriage service over.

So Katherine and Ned, with Jane beside them, stood by the bed in front of this strange priest, who at once opened his book and gabbled through the service. So soon as he had pronounced the couple man and wife, Lady Jane thanked him and showed him out, giving him ten pounds which she had thoughtfully brought with her, from her own allowance.

When she returned to the chamber, the bride was wearing the three-cornered kerchief or 'frows paste' over her caul in recognition of her status as a married woman. They all drank together, attempted to eat some of the refreshments, and laughed hilariously at the strange little priest with his red beard and guttural voice.

"I could not understand one word he uttered," declared Ned. "Where did you find him, my sweet and clever sister?"

Before Jane could explain, Katherine cried, "Have you seen my ring, Jane?"

She stretched out her hand, on what appeared to be a plain gold wedding-ring, rather thick. Katherine slipped it off her finger, pressed a spring, and the ring opened into five gold links, on which was engraved a verse of Hertford's own composition.

"Listen," cried Katherine, and read:

"*As circles five by art compact show*
but one ring in sight,
So trust united faithful minds with
knot of secret might,
Whose force to break (but greedy
death) no wight possesseth power,
As time and sequels well shall prove;
my ring can say no more."

"A marvel of ingenuity," laughed Jane, "and a pretty posy to boot. I did not know my brother was a writer of verse. But put it back on your finger, Kate. Wear it while you may."

Lady Jane then left the chamber, leaving Lord and Lady Hertford to tumble into bed together. After a brief ecstatic oblivion they were recalled to the world by the noisy shouts of some boatmen outside.

"The tide has risen," said Hertford.

"I must go," cried Katherine.

Hurriedly and awkwardly they dressed, helping each other, for neither had ever dressed before without servants to button and belt them. Then they went downstairs to where Lady Jane waited.

At the watergate, Hertford kissed Katherine tenderly in farewell, then hailed a wherry to take his bride and his sister back to the palace, as the tide was now risen and flowing over the Strand path by which they had come. Half-an-hour later they sat side by side demurely eating their dinner at the Lord Controller's table, but the Lady Katherine took only soup without bread or meat, owing to the faceache which had kept her from joining the Queen's sport.

"It is better," she said, "but not yet quite well, though the swelling had gone down somewhat."

Now that Katherine and Ned were married, their need to be together was desperate. In order to facilitate their secret meetings, it was necessary for Katherine to tell her maid, Mrs Leigh, and Hertford confided in his brother,

Lord Henry Seymour.

As loyal as his sister Jane to their beloved brother, Lord Henry became an accomplice to the clandestine romance, and when meetings between the two were impossible carried letters and presents from Ned to Katherine.

He also witnessed a deed of gift from Lord Hertford to his wife, of land to the value of a thousand pounds. At the time they were all together in Lady Jane's apartment, but immediately the transaction was completed, Lady Jane and Lord Henry left them together for a brief interlude of love-making. As always the lovers remained together until the last possible moment, then parted hurriedly.

"Goodbye my sweet, my dearest love," said Ned, and added, "Take care of your deed," for it was still lying on the table, for all to see. Katherine rolled up the document and put it hastily into a coffer which stood empty upon a blanket chest, before she called Mrs Leigh.

Now that they were truly man and wife, Ned and Katherine became less discreet about their meetings and soon most of the court was aware that something was afoot. The gossip reached the ears of the Queen's secretary, Sir William Cecil, who asked Lord Hertford bluntly whether there was goodwill between him and the Lady Katherine Grey.

Lord Hertford answered stoutly, "There is no such thing," but the astute Cecil was far from convinced. He determined to nip the affair in the bud by sending Hertford abroad to accompany his own son, Thomas, who was to take up some legal studies. Lord Hertford was unable to refuse for fear the matter was laid before the Queen, and she would discover the marriage.

On a cold morning in early March, when the Queen had taken to her bed with a chill, Katherine and Jane took boat to Cannon Row. A blustering wind had made the journey far from pleasant and they were glad when they reached the shelter and warmth of Hertford's apartments. A fire burned brightly on the hearth and they drew near to it to drink the mulled wine which had been prepared for them. But Lady Jane was taken with a severe fit of coughing and Lady Katherine felt suddenly and unaccountably sick. In fact, both his visitors were so far from well that Hertford felt that it was no time to break the unwelcome news of his imminent departure for Paris.

He should have told them at once, for his passport was lying on a table and it was seen by his sister Jane, who missed nothing.

"Where are you going, that you need a passport?" she demanded.

"To France, with Sir William Cecil's son, Thomas," he was forced to answer.

"Oh, no, you cannot leave me!" Katherine cried, and burst into a great passion of tears.

"Hush, my sweet, be calm," Hertford soothed. "I tell you, there is as yet no date fixed for my going. It is not certain that I must go."

"But here is your passport."

"Sir William Cecil commanded that I made myself ready to accompany Thomas, but it may not be for some time yet."

"You must not leave me now," Katherine said between sobs, "for I think — I think I am with child."

"Oh, no!" cried Lady Jane. "Oh, no! Are you sure of this?"

"No," answered Katherine, "I am not sure, but I — I am afraid so."

"Then there is no remedy for it. The Queen must be told how the matter stands."

"We must abide by it and trust to the Queen's mercy," agreed Hertford.

"Not yet. Let us wait a little until I am quite certain."

Lady Jane and Lady Katherine took boat and returned to the palace, depressed by the news of Hertford's likely departure for France, worried over the possibility of Katherine's pregnancy, and both feeling very unwell.

Next day Katherine had an urgent desire to see her friend, so worried and distraught did she feel, both over the possibility of her own pregnancy, and her husband's imminent departure for France.

The first fine careless rapture of their marriage had given way to fear and uncertainty. But Jane would know what to do. Jane would be reassuring and steadfast. Alas, Jane's place at table was empty. Lady Jane Seymour was tossing and turning on her bed in a high fever.

"Have you sent for a doctor?" asked Lady Katherine, to the maid who was putting cold towels on Lady Jane's burning forehead.

"He has been sent for, but it seems that he is away from home and we must find another."

Another woman entered the bed-chamber and said, "Her Majesty has been informed of my lady's sickness. She is sending her own doctor at once."

The Queen's doctor bled Lady Jane so soon as he arrived, and for a time she seemed easier, but next day the fever was as high as ever, and soon Lady Jane lapsed into unconsciousness.

Katherine knelt by her friend's bedside and her tears fell.

"Oh Jane, Jane," she cried, "do not desert me. I have no one to turn to but you."

But Lady Jane did not hear her, and presently her spirit quietly ebbed from her body.

Her death was a terrible shock to Katherine. Jane had been a true friend to her, and she was inconsolablc. Queen Elizabeth, too, was genuinely grieved, for Lady Jane Seymour had been one of her favourite ladies. Indeed, she was well beloved by all the court.

She was buried in Westminster Abbey in great state. According to the Queen's command, all the ladies of the royal household, with their attendants, followed the bier from the palace, escorted by fourscore lords and gentlemen of the court. A great banner of arms was borne by a herald before the corpse. The procession was met by the full choir from the Abbey, with two hundred persons in deep mourning.

The procession passed through streets lined with crowds of silent and sympathetic spectators, the men all with their heads bared, for the citizens of London were ready to grieve when their beloved Queen grieved; to share her sorrow as they shared her mirth. And they loved pageantry.

Lady Katherine felt desolate as she left the Abbey, heart-broken for the loss of her dearest friend as well as her confederate. Now she had nobody to turn to, and she felt that the eyes of all the court were turned knowingly and accusingly upon her.

She must see Ned at once and be comforted by him. Accordingly she sent for her maid, Mrs Leigh, and gave her a note to take to Lord Hertford. Distracted, she could think of no other place for their meeting than the apartment so lately occupied by Lady Jane Seymour. But Lady Jane Seymour was no longer there to chaperone them and Katherine gave Mrs Leigh orders to remain outside on guard lest anyone should seek to enter. How this was to be prevented, Katherine left to Mrs Leigh, who paced up and down the Maidens' Bower in such a fever of anxiety as could only advertise the lovers' clandestine meeting.

Inside the apartment, Katherine waited anxiously. The room already looked ownerless. Lady Jane Seymour had been fond of music, but now her lute was missing, also her embroidery frame, and all the evidence of occupation was gone. Katherine paced about despondently, the bareness of the room reminding her of her dear friend's death, and her own solitariness. How happy they had all been together here. All at once, she remembered the deed of gift her husband had presented to her and which she had thrust into a coffer on a blanket chest. The chest was still there, but the coffer was missing. She must make enquiry about it, and recover the deed at once. But now Ned entered the room, and Katherine flew to him. In his embrace all fears and sorrows were temporarily forgotten.

But there was more sorrow in store. Presently, Lord Hertford said, "I have bad tidings for you, my love. Tomorrow I depart for Paris."

"Tomorrow! Oh, no, Ned, you must not leave me now."

"I will soon return, have no fear. Be patient, sweet Kate and all will be well. In the meantime, my Lord Cecil has arranged for me to accompany his son Thomas, who is about to start his legal studies. So soon as he is well installed, I will come back to you, and we will together inform her Majesty of our marriage. Then all this secrecy will be over. But now, my dearest, for a little while, farewell."

So, far from comforting his wife, Lord Hertford left her more dismayed and lonely than ever. The matter of the mislaid deed of gift was completely forgotten in this new distress. That night, Mrs Leigh, while combing out Katherine's tawny curls said diffidently, "My lady, I have something to ask you."

"What is it you wish to say?"

"My mother is gravely ill. I beg you to allow me to leave the court and spend a little time with her."

"You wish to leave me, too?"

"My mother is likely to die, madam."

Katherine was silent for a few moments, then said wearily, "Go then. I would not have you stay against your will."

Mrs Leigh departed next day.

The streets of the city were freshly sanded and gravelled and the houses hung with cloth of arras, rich carpets and silk. Most magnificent of all was the Chepe, hung from one end to the other with cloth of gold and silver and fine velvets of every colour. For her Majesty the Queen was riding by en route for her summer progress through Essex into the heart of Suffolk.

At last she came, acclaimed on all sides, riding through streets lined with all the crafts of London in their liveries, in her new coach, a great wagonette with carved canopy and waving plumes. The Lord Mayor, bearing the sceptre, followed by the aldermen in scarlet robes, escorted it as far as Whitechapel.

Accompanying the Queen in her coach sat Lady Katherine Grey, looking a little pale, perhaps, but beautiful as ever, and elegant in an enormous farthingale which concealed the swelling of her belly.

Everywhere the people cheered; through the streets of London to the country villages, where men and women came running to their doors to see the lumbering coach and its surrounding cavalcade of horsemen. The children, not content to stand and stare, ran alongside, laughing and tumbling, until their little legs could carry them no further.

On they went, by way of Wanstead and Loughton Hall to the Queen's bower at Havering, and here they rested two days. Pyrgo, the estate of Lord John Grey,

Katherine's uncle, was adjacent and the Queen decided to pay him a visit, but Lady Katherine was so conscious of her increasing girth due to her now undoubted pregnancy, that she shrank from meeting anybody who had not seen her recently, fearing her changed appearance would be all too obvious. So she pleaded a violent headache and skulked in the alleys and quarters of the garden of the Bower, which was all laid out and set with quickset and sweetbriar, cherry and apple. It was a sweet place set amidst pleasant woods high upon a hill, and from the topmost windows of the Bower, boats could be seen to pass, up and down the Thames.

Mrs Leigh had not returned from the country where she had gone, ostensibly, to visit her sick mother. But the Lady Mary, had agreed, not without some reluctance, that old Mrs Ellen, now her personal attendant, should accompany her sister on this progress.

Mrs Ellen, who had been present at the execution of Lady Jane, shook her head as she let out bodices and petticoats for her mistress in the privacy of the bedchamber, and wondered anxiously what fate was in store for the lovely Lady Katherine.

Delightful as the Bower at Havering was, her Majesty was anxious to continue her travels, and soon they were on the road again, stopping next at Lord William Petre's place at Ingatestone. The journey was not a long one, but Lady Katherine was feeling sick and Mrs Ellen urged her to retire to bed immediately they arrived.

"Would that I could, Nell, but I dare not. Lord Robert Dudley has brought his actors down, and we are to watch a play in the inner courtyard before we retire."

"Lack-a-day, mistress, you cannot go on much longer with this journey, or the coach will shake the babe right out of you, at her Grace's feet!"

"Oh, Nell, that is what I have been fearing most, ever since I felt it quicken in my womb."

"Then you *must* confess to her Majesty. You cannot go on much longer or this journey will do for you and the babe as well."

"I will tell her, Nell, soon, but not this

day. I must see Dudley's players tonight, come what will."

Her Majesty was well pleased with the play and very merry that night. She particularly commended one of the young actors, Will Shakespeare, who had also composed the piece, and after its performance, by the Queen's command, Lord Robert Dudley sought him out and presented him to her Majesty. All this would have been most pleasant to the Lady Katherine, who loved nothing better than a play, had it not been for her condition and the fear it caused her,

On went the Queen relentlessly, next to Newhall, one of the seats of her grandfather, Sir Thomas Boleyn, where her father, King Henry had often visited to woo her ill-fated mother, Anne Boleyn.

Next Colchester, where her Grace was introduced to a delicacy quite new to her, a shellfish called an oyster. Queen Bess, contrary to her usual frugal habits of eating, consumed an inordinate quantity of oysters, and boisterously called upon her ladies and gentlemen to do likewise. Not to have done so would have shown up her Majesty for a glutton, and so her courtiers all swallowed their oysters by the dozen, tipping them down their throats straight out of the shells, exactly as the Queen was doing. This led to a night of misery for Lady Katherine, with whom the oysters disagreed mightily, but they had no ill effect on the Queen, who continued on her merry way to Harwich.

Since the heat of summer was now at its fiercest, the sea breezes at this pretty little port were most welcome, and the Lady Katherine was not the only one to hope her Majesty would tarry here awhile. But they were soon on their way again, lumbering over rough roads to Gyppeswich.

Lady Katherine sat in a corner, bolstered by silken cushions, her feet braced against the floor of the wagon, her teeth clenched to prevent herself from vomiting. Suppose the child should be born now, as her old nurse had predicted, right at the feet of her virgin Queen. It was unthinkable. But at last they arrived at Gyppeswich and the Queen still had no knowledge of her lady-in-waiting's condition.

Tired, sick, and apprehensive, Lady Katherine threw herself upon her bed. "What shall I do, what shall I do, Nell?" she moaned. "If only Ned were here to stand by me."

Mrs Ellen pursed her lips and said nothing. There was only one piece of advice to give and this she had already given. The Queen must be told, and that at once.

"Ned, Ned," whispered Lady Katherine, "why are you not here by my side?"

Lord Hertford, as it so happened, was at this time, enjoying himself prodigiously in Paris. Mr Thomas Cecil, the studious youth whom he had accompanied, ostensibly to help him with his studies, had sent complaints to his father, Lord Cecil, that his work and meditations were considerably disturbed and interrupted by the gaieties and jaunts organized by Lord Hertford. Lord Cecil turned a deaf ear to his son's complaints.

It was close and airless in Lady Katherine's chamber. Mrs Ellen brought a basin and towel and bathed her mistress's tear-stained face. She had discarded her dress and petticoats, and was lying half-naked on the bed, her figure so swollen and distorted in her pregnancy that it was amazing her condition was still a secret. Mrs Ellen helped her into her night gown.

"Try and sleep now, madam," she advised, "and in the morning, when you are fresh, when the Queen has rested and is most amiable, you *must* face her. There is no help for it. She must be told."

"I cannot tell her. I will not," cried Katherine.

"If you do not, she will discover it for herself," the old woman said tartly, for she too, was tired, and weary of this situation. "Sleep now, madam, and make up your mind to tell the Queen tomorrow."

Lady Katherine slept fitfully, the child, active in her womb, constantly arousing her apprehension. Was it going to be born now? She felt entirely alone and helpless, ignorant of the details of birth, afraid of the agony, and terrified above all, of the Queen's fury.

If the baby was to be born, here and

now, what should she do, how conceal it? And how continue in this tortuous progress? She had come to the end of her endurance. She could not continue in this agony of apprehension another day, another hour, not another minute. She must have help now — now before her child was born.

The Queen must be approached, her forgiveness must be craved. The thought of the Queen's anger was paralysing. Katherine could not face her. Somebody else must inform her Majesty, somebody to whom she would be more sympathetic. But whom? There was only one person who could do no wrong in the eyes of Queen Elizabeth — her master of the horse, Robert Dudley. By day and by night, he was close to her side, sleeping in a chamber communicating with hers. Lord Robert Dudley must help. There was nobody else she could turn to. After all, her sister had been married to his brother. Surely this connection gave him some slight responsibility for her? There was nobody else to whom she was connected. And Robert Dudley could persuade the Queen, if anybody could, that this love-match was no heinous crime. But supposing her labour should start before she had told Robert, begged him to intercede for her? There was no time to be lost, not an instant. Robert Dudley must be told now, this very minute.

Lady Katherine rose, and bare-footed and in her night attire she stumbled into Lord Robert Dudley's bedchamber. By the light of the moon which shone through a narrow casement, she could make out his dark hair and handsome features, and the long thick lashes which rested lightly upon his cheeks as he slept. Softly she whispered his name. He did not stir. Distraught, she fell upon her knees and acting upon some strange impulse, scarce knowing what she did, began to cover his face with kisses.

He started up, muttering, "Bess, what would you?" Then, as he awoke fully, he cried in astonishment and consternation, "In heaven's name, what brings you here? Are you mad?"

"I — I" began Katherine, then burst into such a storm of tears that not a word could she utter.

"Be quiet, madam, for mercy's sake. You will rouse her Majesty with your noise. Whatever is your plight, I have nought to do with it, and I would not have the Queen think otherwise."

"You must help me. You must tell the queen — "

"Tell her? Tell her what?"

"That I am married to Lord Hertford, and will shortly bear his child."

"What? You are married to Hertford! When and how did this take place?"

"Secretly, at his house, just before Christmas."

"And you expect me to acquaint the Queen with this infamous story? Why tell me? Why not go to her yourself?"

"I dare not. She will be so angry. But she will listen to you, and she will have mercy on me if you plead for me."

"I plead for you! I will have nothing to do with you. Why should I risk angering her Majesty by relating your sorry affairs? Go! Get out of here, before we are surprised. A fine figure I should cut if you were discovered here. The brat would be mine, by implication. Get out of here, I say."

Weeping bitterly, Katherine left Robert Dudley's bedchamber and, too distraught to go back to her own bed and wait until the morning, she now stumbled into Bess Hardwick's bedroom.

Bess must help her. Was it not at her wedding, oh, a lifetime ago it seemed, that Katherine had first ridden with Lord Hertford. The Duke and Duchess of Suffolk had given Bess Hardwick, or Mistress Saintlow, as she now was, a fine wedding at Bradgate Park, in the name of friendship, and Katherine had later stood godmother to their first child. Why had Katherine not thought of her before? Of course she was the person to be told, who would help. She was a woman of the world. Surely she would know some way out.

Bess Hardwick resented this interruption to her night's sleep as much if not more than Robert Dudley had done. She listened coldly while Katherine poured out her story incoherently between sobs, then turned upon her indignantly. "You wicked slut," she cried. "Do you expect me to believe that Lord Hertford has lawfully wed you? A likely story!"

"It is true. I swear it is true. I am his wife and he is the father of the child I am to bear."

"Then why drag me into your sorry affairs? Do you think I want to share her Majesty's anger?"

"I cannot face her. You *must* tell her for me. I dare not," sobbed Katherine.

Mrs Saintlow then burst into hysterical tears herself, and begged Katherine to leave her, for she had no mind to get mixed up in the affair.

Lady Katherine returned to her own room, exhausted by her emotions, and creeping into bed fell into a heavy sleep. When she awakened the sun was high in the heavens, and the Queen had been told the whole story.

Upon reflection, Lord Robert Dudley had decided it would be best for her to hear about it from his lips rather than anybody else's, so he had obtained a private audience with Elizabeth and related the facts. The Queen was livid. Even Robert Dudley, who knew the Queen in all her moods, had witnessed her sudden rages, had even on occasion dodged the slipper she would pull from her foot and fling across the room, was unprepared for the tempest his story evoked. Elizabeth raged and stormed, and swore that she would see the Lady Katherine dead rather than have a child of this mis-conceived alliance as heir to the throne of England.

"Then let us put this unborn brat's nose out of joint," cried Robert. "Let me give you an heir to the throne, sweet Bess. There is nothing would please your people more than to see you happily married."

The moment for this proposal was ill-timed. "Marry you!" screamed the Queen. "Are you mad? Do you know what is said of you in the taverns and at the fairs? That you murdered your wife to further your ambitions. Oh no, Robert, I cannot marry you. You I can only love."

The Queen's rage left her and she fell into a fit of melancholy from which she presently roused herself to say, "Have this girl sent to the Tower at once. I do not wish to see her or to hear her excuses. These she must save for her trial."

10

KATHERINE was put into a litter and sent back to London, the faithful Mrs Ellen riding on horseback behind. Katherine was calm, almost cheerful, so great was her relief now that her secret was out. She would have her baby, Ned would return from Paris, and in time the Queen would forgive her. She had done no wrong except to marry secretly and without the Queen's permission. Surely this was not so terrible. Katherine was forgetting her position as next in succession to the throne of England. Not so Mrs Ellen, who remembered the other young mistress she had served in the Tower of London; remembered that for all Queen Mary's fondness for Lady Jane her life had not been spared. But Queen Elizabeth was not fond of Lady Katherine. She would spare her no mercy. Mrs Ellen pictured herself standing on the scaffold a second time and watching another young head severed from its body and rolling in the blood-stained straw.

Lady Katherine's cheerfulness was sustained until the door shut fast upon her and she realized that she was indeed a prisoner in the Tower as her sister had been, and her father and her uncle, and indeed, her husband's father. They had all died. Beheaded. Katherine put her hands to her own slender neck as if to protect it from this awful fate.

"Nelly," she whispered, "what will become of me? What will they do?"

"Do not fret, mistress," the old nurse comforted her, assuming a cheerfulness she was very far from feeling. "The Queen is angry now, terribly angry, but her rages never last for long. She will forgive you, never fear."

"But my baby, Nelly? Is my child to be born in here?" She looked round wildly, at the stone floor and bare walls, and the narrow bed.

"It looks like it, madam. It looks very much like it to me. Your time is very near now, but have no fear. Your old Nelly will look after you. All will be well. Rest now. You must be very weary after your long journey."

Katherine *was* very weary and with Mrs Ellen's comforting words in her ears was soon fast asleep, in spite of the hardness of her prison bed. Next day she was confronted by the lieutenant of the Tower, Sir Edward Warner, who had been instructed to find out how many people were privy to the affair. It was necessary that Lady Katherine's marriage should not be acknowledged. By the will of King Henry VIII, her mother's uncle, her claim to the throne preceded that of Mary, Queen of Scots, Elizabeth's cousin, and the Queen was well aware that foreign suitors, in despair of winning her own hand, were looking speculatively towards Katherine. If she produced a son, Spain might well support his claim to the throne, in rivalry to France and Scotland's Queen Mary. Indeed, there might even be some within her own court who had engineered this marriage deliberately. Fornication would have been a lesser crime.

Sir Edward Warner, torn between his duty, and pity for this lovely but luckless lady, questioned her gently and Lady Katherine poured out the whole story of her love for Lord Hertford, from Mrs Saintlow's wedding day, when she and Ned had galloped together on a soft, summer's night, and she had saved his life from the wolf.

"I had no intention of deceiving her Majesty," she declared. "I always meant, and so did Ned, to gain the Queen's consent to our marriage. My mother approved of our union and promised to speak for us. She wrote a letter to the Queen, interceding for us."

"Where is this letter?" asked Sir Edward.

Katherine shook her head despairingly. "I do not know," she admitted. "It never reached the Queen."

"Who was the minister who married you?" was the next question.

"I never heard his name."

"What was he like?"

Katherine remembered this very well — remembered their gaiety over the little priest with his guttural accent.

"He was a short man in a long gown of black cloth faced with budge fur," she said, "and his collar was turned down after the sort that the ministers used to wear, of the German sect, when they first returned to England after the death of Queen Mary. He was a high-complexioned man with a red beard," she added, and she began to giggle hysterically at the memory of this priest.

"Who witnessed this marriage?" was the next question.

"My lord's sister, the Lady Jane Seymour," Katherine gulped.

"None other?"

"No," she whispered, and began to cry.

Suddenly she realized the hopelessness of her position. She was truly married, but there had been only one witness. She was dead and the priest was not to be found. She recollected Hertford's man passing them along the river bank. He had been sent away deliberately, and no servant at all had been present at the ceremony.

"I have a ring," said Katherine. "This is the ring my husband gave me, and I have worn it ever since."

She produced a ring threaded through

a ribbon worn round her neck beneath her bodice.

"It has five links," she said, and pressed the spring to reveal the five links of gold, engraved with Hertford's verse.

Then Katherine remembered the deed of gift which Hertford had given to her soon after the marriage, but she could not produce it.

"It was written on a parchment," she said, "which I put in a coffer, hurriedly. I meant to retrieve it later, but I — I forgot. I do not know what is become of it."

"But you must know where to find this valuable document. Surely you locked it up somewhere safely?"

"I left it in Lady Jane Seymour's boudoir, which was dismantled after her death. I meant to make enquiry for the coffer with the deed inside it, but I was distracted by Lord Hertford's departure for Paris. Mrs Leigh — my maid, Mrs Leigh — " Katherine's voice trailed off hopelessly.

"Yes, yes, your maid, Mrs Leigh? Can she help you? She knew of your marriage?"

"Yes."

"Then we must send for her at once. Where is this Mrs Leigh?"

"I do not know."

"What?"

"Her mother was ill, she said, and I gave her permission to visit her mother. She never returned. I do not know how to find her."

"So," said Sir Edward Warner, shaking his head, "you are married, by a priest whose name and whereabouts you have no knowledge of. You can produce no witness to your union. You have a deed of gift from your husband but this has disappeared, and your maid, who was privy to all these doings, has left your service."

In answer, Katherine could only weep.

"Madam," said Mrs Ellen, to her mistress, who lay apathetically upon her narrow prison bed, "your husband is here."

"Here?" cried Katherine. "You mean he has returned to England? Then he will make all things right with her Majesty, and we will soon be together as man and wife."

"He is here, madam, in the White Tower. He was arrested so soon as he arrived at Dover, and escorted to London under a strong guard."

"So he is a prisoner, too. Oh, Nelly! What shall we do? Whatever will become of us?"

Mrs Ellen could give no answer, no comfort to her young mistress. In her mind all the time was the memory of Katherine's sister Jane, and that last awful morning on the scaffold. Was she to accompany Lady Katherine to her death, too? Lady Jane's only crime, if crime it had been, was in obedience to her parents wishes. Lady Katherine had wantonly followed the dictates of her own heart. Would death on the block be her lot, too?

The next week Lord Hertford was questioned by Sir Edward Warner, the Privy Council, and a formidable array of lawyers and divines. He faced his questioners with manliness, freely avowing his marriage and professing passionate love for his wife. His evidence agreed with Lady Katherine's exactly, and he recited by heart the verses he had made up and had engraved upon the wedding ring. His description of the priest tallied with that given by Katherine, but like her, he was unable to give the man's name.

He had forgotten it, he said, or probably he never heard it. His dear sister had found the priest and witnessed the ceremony and she was in her grave.

The earl was plagued with questions for several days; he was browbeaten and intimidated in every way that could be devised and his evidence was made to include an exact description of his love-making, but he never deviated from his story. Great search was apparently made for the divine, but he was not forthcoming and as he had been invisible to all but the bride and bridegroom and the bridesmaid, the Privy Council chose to assume that he had never existed.

Mrs Saintlow and Lord Hertford's brother, Lord Henry Seymour were also questioned and Lord Hertford's servants, but no conclusion was arrived at and no announcement made about the validity or otherwise of the marriage.

Lady Katherine, pacing in agony to and

fro in her prison cell, had little concern for the conclusions of the Privy Council, for her labour had begun. Mrs Ellen bustled about in excited anticipation, setting out borrowed bowl and towels. From the Lieutenant of the Tower down to the veriest mite of a warder's child, making daisy chains on Tower Green, there was sympathy and interest for the lovely lady who was about to give birth to what might well be the heir to the throne of England, in the stark discomfort of the Bell Tower.

Perhaps the Queen's secretary, Lord Cecil, waiting at Greenwich Palace, secretly hoped that Lady Katherine would die in childbirth and her baby, too, thus relieving him of his dilemma. Perhaps Queen Elizabeth hoped so, too, but in this they were disappointed, for the Lady Katherine was safely delivered of a fine, healthy boy.

Sir Edward visited her in her cell so soon as she had recovered from her ordeal. "Show Sir Edward my son," she commanded Mrs Ellen, who proudly brought the baby for the Lieutenant's inspection.

"A lovely child," he commented, peering down at the red, crumpled little new-born face.

Katherine smiled blissfully. Nobody could take this from her, her pride and pleasure in her baby — hers and Ned's.

"I am distressed that you are confined in such discomfort," said Sir Edward Warner.

"It is nothing to me now," answered Lady Katherine. "I am content — I would be content, but for one thing."

"And that is?"

"I long to show my baby to his father."

"That is not possible, madam."

"But he is so near. I am told that he is imprisoned in the White Tower."

"That is so."

"Then could he not be brought here, under guard, to see his son?"

"I have the strictest instructions, madam, that there is to be no meeting between you and your hus — between you and Lord Hertford. I am sorry to disappoint you, but I dare not do otherwise."

"I understand, Sir Edward," said

Katherine. She closed her eyes wearily, and a tear escaped and trickled down her white cheek.

The Lieutenant of the Tower looked down at her, lying on her hard bed. He looked at the bare walls and the cold flagstoned floor, and left the cell, full of compassion and a desire to help his prisoner. A few days later he sent two servants with a coffer for Lady Katherine. Mrs Ellen unpacked it.

"Look madam," she cried, "some tapestries for your walls, and a silk quilt for your bed."

"Show me, Nelly."

"Here you are, madam. A quilt of red and gold stripes. It is faded, forsooth, and a little torn."

"It will do. What else has Sir Edward sent to me?"

Mrs Ellen held up the tapestries, which were old and coarse.

"Beggars can't be choosers," said Lady Katherine. "Is there anything else?"

"A tester for your bed, madam."

"It was kind of him. We will use his presents."

A few days later, Sir Edward Warner

came again to Lady Katherine's prison. It looked more comfortable, albeit shabby, but Katherine was sitting on her bed uncomfortably, feeding her baby.

"It is scandalous," he muttered, "that there is so little comfort for you."

The next day his servants arrived with an enormous and ornate chair of cloth of gold cased with crimson velvet which had at one time graced the state apartments. This was followed by some old Turkey matting to put on the stone floor. Still apologetic for these sparse comforts, Sir Edward next sent two old footstools of green velvet, faded and stained.

"The very stools," said old nurse Ellen, "that your great-uncle used to rest his swelled and festering leg upon."

"Ah, yes, King Henry," said Lady Katherine. "I do not remember him. What was he like, Nelly?"

"A very handsome gentleman when he was young, but he suffered greatly before he died. All puffed and swollen with the dropsy, he was, and his wife, his last wife, Queen Katherine Parr, would kneel by his side by the hour, applying fomentations to relieve his pain and soothing him by her gentle presence. Sometimes, in the last months of his life, he would lay his sore leg on her lap in the presence of the whole court."

"I would that Queen Katherine Parr had made him change his will," said Lady Katherine wearily. "It is by his command that I am in this unhappy state."

"How so, madam?"

"Had I not been named in his will as heiress to the throne after his son and daughters and my sister Jane, I could have married whom I pleased, instead of languishing here, imprisoned and parted from my true husband."

"Have patience, madam. The Queen will relent and release you presently."

"If I could only think so," sighed Katherine. "Never mind, Nelly, we have a champion in Sir Edward Warner. What will his next present be, do you suppose?"

It was a cushion of purple velvet, rubbed and shabby, but the servant who brought it was accompanied by his daughter. She was a shy little girl who only hung her head when Lady Katherine asked her if she would like to see the baby; but in her fist she held a bunch of drooping gillyflowers and these she pushed into Lady Katherine's lap before running back to her father and half-hiding herself behind him.

"Are they for me? How kind of you to give me your flowers," said Lady Katherine. "Did you pick them from your garden?"

The child blushed and nodded and looked as though there was something she wished to say, but shyness held her tongue-tied until she left the apartment, clinging to her father's hand.

"Poor little flowers," said Lady Katherine, "are you to be prisoners, too? You are drooping already. Here, Nelly, put them in water before they die. Have we a jug that they can stand in?"

As Mrs Ellen took the bunch of flowers and began to arrange them in a bowl, a note fell out. She picked it up and handed it to her mistress.

"What is it, Nelly?"

"I cannot say, madam. It fell from the flowers."

Lady Katherine unfolded the paper, her heart beating fast as she recognized her husband's handwriting. The note was short. It said,

'*To my dearest wife, Katherine, to tell her that I love her with all my heart and long to see her and our son. Do not despair, for one day soon we shall all be together. From your devoted husband,*
Ned.'

Lady Katherine raised the note to her lips and her tears fell fast.

Sir Edward Warner was kindness itself to mother and child, and came often to see them. He would have granted Lady Katherine's dearest wish, to show her son to his father, had he dared, but these prisoners were too important for him to contravene her Majesty's express orders. He turned a blind eye, however, to the visits of his servant's little daughter, and soon she was acting as go-between for the lovers, regularly bringing and taking notes and posies from one to another.

Lady Katherine was not entirely forgotten by the outside world, for Adrian Stokes, her mother's widower, contrived to send the monkey of which she had been so fond in those far-away days at Bradgate Park. It evoked bitter-sweet memories of other happier days for her, but for the baby the monkey was a source of great amusement, and he was soon chortling merrily at its antics. It loved to climb up the walls, clinging to the tapestries, which, already worn and old, were soon reduced to rags.

Although the legitimacy of the baby was still in question, Sir Edward Warner gained permission from the Queen for him to be christened. Lord Hertford, peering from his prison window, had a brief glimpse of his wife and son as the little procession took its way to the chapel of St Peter-ad-Vincula on Tower Green, where the baby received the name and title of Edward Seymour, Viscount Beauchamp. No living relatives, except his mother, witnessed the ceremony, but it took place over the tombs of the headless bodies of seven of his forbears. These included his father's father, Lord Somerset; his father's uncle, Admiral Seymour; his mother's sister, Lady Jane Grey; her father, the Duke of Suffolk, and her uncle Lord Thomas Grey; his mother's brother-in-law, Lord Guildford Dudley, and Dudley's father, the Duke of Northumberland.

Lady Katherine hoped against hope that the Queen's pardon would soon follow the baby's christening, but months passed without any decision being made. A rumour spread that the priest had been found but was being kept out of the way, in order to bastardize the child, and keep him from succeeding to the throne.

At last the Queen instructed Lord Parker, the Archbishop of Canterbury, to re-examine the prisoners and to give judgement on their pretended marriage. They were conducted to Lambeth under guard, and were not allowed to speak to anyone or to one another.

Every intimate detail of their marriage was again probed and corroborated by the prisoners. Hertford agreed that he had not made a will in Katherine's favour, only given her the deed of gift, and this was lost. It was a thin story, no doubt about that. Who would forget all about so important and valuable a document as the deed of gift? How was it possible that the marriage ceremony was performed by an entirely unknown priest? Had he been conjured out of a hat and spirited away into thin air?

After the relentless cross-questioning, Katherine herself began to wonder whether she had dreamt it all. The ring, now worn defiantly on her finger, was the only evidence of the actual marriage ceremony and this was not sufficient proof. Katherine and Ned were taken back to their prisons, where they each waited despondently for the decision of the Archbishop's commission.

On a May morning, some eight months after Katherine's arrival at the Tower, Sir Edward Warner took himself to her apartments. He was heavy-hearted and reluctant to carry the message which he had just received from the Queen herself. He found Katherine quite merry and playing with her little boy on the floor.

"See how fast he crawls," she cried, "and he pulls himself up by the chair and stands. Soon he will be walking."

"He is a fine boy," agreed Sir Edward.

"But he is pale," said Katherine anxiously, "and the sun is shining.

He has committed no crime. I would that he might take some exercise in the fresh air. It is not good for him to be cooped up forever in these four walls."

"His crime was in his birth," answered Sir Edward sombrely.

"It was no crime," protested his mother sharply.

"He has been pronounced a bastard, his birth unlawful and illegitimate, the result of carnal copulation between yourself and the Earl of Hertford."

"Who says so?"

"The Queen herself has informed me that these are the findings of the Archbishop's commission."

"And the sentence?" whispered Katherine.

"Continued imprisonment."

"For how long?"

The term was for life, but this Sir Edward Warner found it quite impossible to communicate.

"During the Queen's pleasure," he answered. "Be of good cheer. The Queen will relent. Be patient, and when the Queen herself marries and has a child, which surely will not be long, you will be forgiven."

"If only it could be so," sighed Katherine.

"And this very day you shall take your child out to enjoy the warmth of the sun."

So Katherine was comforted and she walked out on Tower Green with Mrs Ellen and her baby in the May sunshine. With the optimism of youth, she believed that soon her crime would be forgiven, and they would all be able to leave the Tower. They would live in a little cottage in the country, miles away from the court and they would all be blissfully happy, and Queen Elizabeth could forget their very existence. Yes, that is what they would do.

Musing thus, Lady Katherine came to the very spot where her sister Jane had been beheaded seven years earlier. Her mood of optimism left her, and she felt a great sadness for Jane and marvelled at her fortitude. How brave she had been! Lady Katherine turned to the nurse and found that Mrs Ellen's old face was creased with sorrow, and her tears were spattering on to the face of the baby she held in her arms, as she recalled the tragedy of Lady Jane's death. The baby was crying, the fickle spring sunshine had clouded over and a chill wind was blowing.

"Let's go indoors," said Katherine sadly. It was all a dream that could never come true, this cottage for her and Ned. They would linger on in the Tower, imprisoned separately, never to meet, until they died. Perhaps it would be a mercy if they all had their heads chopped off at once, to spare them this lingering death in life.

Mrs Ellen, ashamed of her own grief, did her best to comfort her young mistress. "Her Majesty will pardon you in time, madam," she said, "and at least you can now take the air with your child. That is something."

"Yes, Nelly, that is something," sighed Katherine, and from this time she spent part of each day walking on Tower Green, Mrs Ellen carrying the baby. Lord Hertford could see her from his window in the White Tower and longed to walk with her and to see his son. He waited and watched for them every day.

Sir Edward Warner, visiting him, was touched when he found Lord Hertford so constantly by his window, eager for a glimpse of his wife and child.

Surely it would do no harm to allow a meeting between these star-crossed lovers. Since they were not to be released and their child was declared a bastard, what could it matter what happened to them behind the walls of the Tower? They would soon be entirely forgotten by the outside world. Very well then, some compassion must be shown to them. The prisoner should take some exercise.

And so one morning as Katherine walked upon the grass she saw her husband coming towards her. They fell into each other's arms and kissed and wept.

"Here is your son," said Katherine, proudly presenting the baby.

"Poor child," cried Hertford, "to begin his life in prison."

"He is quite happy," said Katherine. "He lacks for nothing."

"And you, my dearest?"

"I lack your love," she answered, and

they embraced again. All too soon it was time for them to part. This meeting agitated Katherine very much. She longed for Ned, and felt extremely dejected when she was once more locked in her apartments in the Bell Tower.

She dreamed about her husband, dreamed that she was in his arms, and waking, saw him standing by her bedside. It could not be true. She must be dreaming still. It was a trick of her imagination, her eyes were deceiving her.

He spoke her name, softly, tenderly.

"Ned! Is it true? Is it really you, in the flesh, and not some dream. Oh, tell me it is not a dream, that I shall not wake to find you gone."

"I am here with you, my love."

"But how is this? How came you here?"

"Hush, my darling." His lips were on hers, his arms were round her. "I am here, here with you at last."

"Do not question how I got here," he said, and crushed her to him, silencing her with his lips on hers. They were together at last, and in the bliss of their union, the tragic past slipped away, and the future was non-existent. There was only the present, this glorious moment to be lived rapturously, come what may. All that they had suffered in the past, all that they might have to endure in the future they would barter for this night of bliss. Here, in this bare and shabby cell they were together, and nothing could ever take this night from them. They were caught up in a golden, radiant web of love and happiness. Time must stand still. This moment must never end.

Katherine sighed and slept, her cheek pressed against her husband's cheek, his arms around her.

Katherine was happy. Her baby thrived, the sun shone and Ned contrived to visit her frequently. During that halcyon summer the outside world was forgotten and indeed, appeared to have forgotten them.

Even when she became pregnant again her complacency was unshaken. Having been imprisoned, her marriage disbelieved, and her son declared illegitimate, she felt it mattered little to anybody what happened to her now. Perhaps Sir Edward Warner thought so too. Perhaps he thought that what happened within the Tower was nobody's business so long as the prisoners were not allowed to escape. The only one to feel any real uneasiness at the situation was Lord Hertford, but since there was nothing to be done about it, he kept his qualms to himself.

In the autumn of that year strange rumours were heard concerning the death of Queen Elizabeth. An astrologer named Prestal had predicted her death the following spring, so when she suddenly became violently ill in October, the court was thrown into consternation. She had contracted smallpox and such alarming symptoms occurred that her death was anticipated. Her council kept vigil in her chamber while she lay insensible to all around her. However, after being in a deathlike stupor for four hours she revived and gradually recovered.

Now the question of her succession became of paramount importance to her council, and the following February the majority of the ministers at a

Council meeting named Lady Katherine as successor to the throne. Three days later she gave birth to her second son.

The Queen's wrath was awful. Poor Sir Edward Warner lost his place and was imprisoned in one of his own dungeons.

Lord Hertford was ordered to appear before a Court of the Star Chamber on the triple charge that he had two years before deflowered a virgin of the blood royal in the Queen's house; that he had broken prison in visiting Lady Katherine, and that he had ravished her a second time.

Hertford boldly replied, "I have lawfully contracted marriage with the Lady Katherine and I do not deny that I have passed through the open door of my prison to comfort her."

He was heavily fined and ordered to remain imprisoned during her Majesty's pleasure.

After this there was no question of Katherine and Hertford being able to meet again, but the baby was baptised and named Thomas Seymour.

11

IT was May Day and the apprentices swarming on London Bridge were disappointed to find there was no spectacle for them to cheer or boo; no tilting or jousting or bear-baiting or morris dancing, for the Queen was at Greenwich, still not fully recovered from her malady of the previous autumn. The boys were restive and an argument soon developed among a group of them. They were discussing the case of the Lady Katherine and Lord Hertford.

"Serves them right," said one, "for disobeying Queen Bess."

"They had every right to marry," said a second, "since they were solemnly betrothed to each other."

"That's right," agreed a third. "It was not only their right to wed, but it would have been wrong for either to marry another."

"True enough," it was agreed.

"Likewise," said another apprentice,

"that marriage might be celebrated at any place or hour by any Christian clergyman."

"True, true," roared the lads, "and 'tis cruel wrong to keep them apart and bastardize their babies."

The boys were beginning to enjoy themselves. They had a cause, a just cause to defend. When one of them, brandishing his cudgel ferociously cried, "We'll get them out of there!" they all responded with shouts and shaking of fists and started to run over the bridge and along the embankment towards the Tower. More boys joined in as they swept along until they formed a great body three or four thousand strong. They rushed upon the Tower, yelling and battering upon its outer walls.

The guard was called out, and, mounted and armed, soon diverted the mob, to the great relief of all its frightened inmates, prisoners, warders and lions. But far from dispersing, the crowd of apprentices were further incensed, and on being unable to gain access to the Tower, swept through the city into the suburbs committing outrages in every direction.

At Stratford-atte-Bow the boys swarmed upon a house of correction and completely demolished it, beginning with the roof and then rushing upon the building with their staves and cudgels until the walls crumbled. Only the stout oak timbers, which withstood all attack, were left, but all the prisoners escaped and joined the apprentices.

It was a May Day outrage long to be remembered and talked about. At the court at Greenwich, idle during the Queen's prolonged convalescence, the story lost nothing in the telling and it added to the irritation felt by Queen Elizabeth over the whole episode of Lady Katherine and Lord Hertford, though in truth it was not their fault. The apprentices' indignation over the couple's plight was more an excuse for their exuberance, too long contained at bench and counter, than any genuine concern for the Tower prisoners.

The little Lady Mary had moved out to Greenwich with the court. She was lonely. She missed her sister, Katherine, but more sorely, she missed her dear friend Master Keyes, who had remained at Westminster. So she needed little persuading to accompany the Queen's maid, Blanche Parry, to the jewellers in the Chepe.

They were rowed up the Thames in one of her Majesty's barges and enjoyed the voyage, for although the weather had turned very hot, it was cool and pleasant on the river. They disembarked at the watergate at Westminster Palace, and there was Thomas Keyes, waiting to help them out of the barge and delighted to see them. Lady Mary gave him her hand to help her out, but he leant forward and putting his strong arms round her waist, lifted her bodily from the barge and set her down. She felt the pressure from his arms for long after he had removed them, and was full of warmth and well-being and buoyancy. It was good to see him, and when he offered to escort them to the city the Lady Mary was pleased to allow this, although it was not strictly necessary, as they had men servants with them.

They set out from the palace in a

horse coach which rumbled along the cobbled streets on two broad and high wheels. The streets stank in the hot sunshine. They put pomanders close to their noses and sniffed them to keep out the worst of the stench. The roads were noisy and crowded with a multitude of carts, large and small, conveying beer and coal and wood. There were waggons up from the country, carrying food and passengers, higgledy-piggledy, and there were some very filthy carts which were employed solely for cleansing the streets and carrying manure. The City had looked very different when it was all cleaned and decorated for the Queen's progress, and the citizens all in their Sunday best.

Their errand, to collect a diamond ouch for the Queen's bodice, was soon executed and they started back for the palace. An evil-looking man driving a filthy manure cart jostled against their carriage in the narrow street. Their driver, incensed by this outrage to a royal coach, raised his whip to strike the fellow, but the man suddenly lurched forward and fell from his cart, face downwards on the mucky street. He lay where he had fallen, and some bystanders went to his assistance. They turned him over and exposed his face to view. It was blotched and swollen and was dark purple colour.

"Drive on," cried Master Keyes. "Drive on! It is the plague. We must get these ladies away from here quickly!"

The coachman whipped up his horses and they drove on towards Westminster.

"Could we do nothing for that poor wretch?" asked Lady Mary.

"There was nothing to be done," answered Thomas Keyes gravely. "In a few hours he will be dead. Her Majesty would not thank us for bringing the plague to her palace."

Soon there were reports of more and more people falling victim to the plague, until at least a thousand had perished in London alone. This was a bad outbreak and there was little hope of it abating until the end of the relentlessly hot summer.

The court moved out to Windsor, where it was cooler and pleasant and had not been reached by the epidemic. Lady Mary worried over her sister and the two baby boys, little nephews whom she had never seen. At last she summoned up courage to beg her Majesty to send them away from the foetid city. The Queen agreed at once, somewhat to Lady Mary's surprise. Perhaps Queen Elizabeth feared there would be a renewal of demonstrations for Lady Katherine's release, when alarm about the plague abated.

"We will send them to your uncle at Pyrgo, in Essex," she said, after a little thought.

Lady Mary was overjoyed. By 'them' she assumed that the Queen meant Katherine and her husband and two babies, but this proved not to be the case. Lady Katherine and her baby were to be lodged with her uncle, Lord John Grey, in Essex, and Lord Hertford was to be removed to his mother's house in Middlesex, the other child with him.

This was a clever move on the part of the Queen, for while it would seem that her generous heart had prevailed over her head in releasing the prisoners from the Tower and sending them to their relatives in more salubrious places, in fact they were still to be imprisoned as closely as ever, separately, and without the least chance of meeting each other.

Lord John Grey and his good wife took the air in the pleasant grounds of their seat, Pyrgo, adjacent to the Queen's Bower at Havering.

"Let us sit awhile, my love," he said, indicating a rustic seat, shrouded from the sun, by a gigantic oak.

Lord John was content. His affairs had gone well of late. Without a doubt, the country prospered under good Queen Bess. True, at this moment, the capital was suffering from a bad outbreak of the plague, but here, in the sweet air of the Essex countryside they were immune from infection.

His reverie was interrupted by a serving-man who approached them bearing a missive upon a tray. "My lord," he said, "a messenger from her Majesty's court has delivered this letter to you."

"Her Majesty?" said Lord John, in

some surprise, "What does the Queen want of me?"

"Read it, my dear sir," advised his wife, equably.

Lord John Grey broke the seal of the letter and perused its contents.

"What does it say?" enquired his wife, noting his brows drawn together, irritably. "Are you to attend her Majesty at court?"

"No, no, my dear. Cecil writes to inform me her Majesty desires me to take charge of my niece, Katherine. She is to arrive tomorrow, with her baby son, attended by her women."

"She has been released from the Tower?"

"Yes, on account of the plague, but we are to keep her imprisoned, it seems. The letter says, '*She is to be treated as in custody, not to depart till her Majesty's pleasure be further known, neither to have any conference with any person not of your household, which her Majesty meaneth she should understand as part of her punishment*'. Here's a fine to-do! Are we to keep her under lock and key?"

"She will not try to leave us. Where

else could she go, forsooth? I must have a suite prepared for her and her baby," said Lady Grey, rising from her seat, and leaving her husband to ponder upon the imminent destruction of his peace.

Lady Katherine had been in poor health since the birth of her second child, and she missed Lord Hertford sorely. She missed, too, her visits from poor Sir Edward Warner, incarcerated in one of his own dungeons solely on account of his kindness to her and Lord Hertford. Now she was to be parted from her little son, Edward, as well. As if this was not enough to try her, her beloved pet, Beppo, the monkey had been found dead, inexplicably.

In vain did Mrs Ellen try to pacify her, to point out that the Queen would relent in due course, and they would all be together again. Lady Katherine was devastated by grief but she had no choice but to obey the Queen's command.

Now the time had come for her to leave her little boy. In order to save him distress, Mrs Ellen, who was to remain with him, took him for a walk upon the green, and he had no idea that he was being parted from his mother. From her window Lady Katherine watched the sturdy fair-haired child. She saw him pull away from his nurse's side to chase a raven, and heard his merry laugh.

Sobbing bitterly, she was put into a carriage with her baby and his nursemaid. But before they started off a little figure ran to the carriage, and climbing up, pressed a small packet into Lady Katherine's hand. It was the jailer's little daughter, who had acted as go-between for Hertford and Katherine, and he had sent her a parting present. It was a mourning ring, engraved with a death's head, and the words '*While I live, yours*'.

Her aunt and uncle were much concerned by her woebegone appearance when she arrived at Pyrgo. She was pale and thin, and had no appetite. Lord John forgot the impatience he had felt at the prospect of housing her, and became touched and concerned for her, at meal-times pressing special little tit-bits upon her, to tempt her appetite.

"Good madam, eat something to comfort yourself. You will pine away else," he said to her, genuine concern in his voice.

Lady Katherine tried, but the food choked her. "What is that I hear?" she said, pushing the platter from her. "It sounds like a horn."

"It is indeed a horn, a hunting-horn," replied her uncle. "Her Majesty's Bower at Havering is but half a league from here, and she has brought her court from London to hunt the wild boar in the forest."

"The Queen is here now?" asked Katherine. She visualized the gay hunting party, and the lavish entertainment which would follow, the masques and balls and elaborate dressing-up, which would be taking place so near and yet so far from her. When she was imprisoned in the Tower, the gay life of the court had been another world, far removed from her in her prison. Now it was so near and yet so far, that Lady Katherine realized fully all she had lost. She was an outcast, never more to take her place, her rightful position, in her monarch's court. Soon she would be forgotten entirely, beholden to her uncle, and left to languish. It was a sad fate to be in the Queen's displeasure.

She burst into a torrent of weeping, and rising from the dining-table fled to her own chamber. Flinging herself upon the bed she abandoned herself to grief.

Lord John followed her. He sat upon her bed and stroked her hair.

"Do not distress yourself so," he begged her.

"What sort of a life is this, the Queen's displeasure has brought upon me? I would to God I were dead and buried, but for my husband and my children."

"You are young. You will not always live like this in the Queen's displeasure. She will forgive you, and you will be reunited with your dear lord and your son."

"Would it were so," she replied heavily.

"Come, dry your eyes, and we will each pen a letter to secretary Lord Cecil."

At last Katherine was persuaded that the Queen would pardon her in due course, and she wrote a pitiful letter to the Queen's secretary, in the hope that he would pass her letter on to her Majesty. She expressed her gratitude for being released from the Tower, and begged Cecil to intercede for her with Queen Elizabeth, 'for the obtaining of the Queen's Majesty's most gracious pardon and favour towards me, which with upstretched hands and down bent knees from the bottom of my heart most humbly I crave.'

No answer was received to this obsequious appeal.

Lord John also wrote to Cecil, and when his letter, too was ignored, wrote to Robert Dudley, now Earl of Leicester, but to no avail.

Lady Katherine now approached the Queen directly.

> '*Most gracious Sovereign,*' she wrote, '*I dare not presume to crave pardon for my disobedient and most rash matching of myself without your Highness's consent. I acknowledge myself a most unworthy creature to fail so much your gracious favour as I have done. My just felt misery and continual grief doth teach me daily, more and more, the greatness of my fault, and your princely*

pity increases my sorrow, that I have so forgotten my duty to your Majesty. This is my great torment of mind. May it therefore please your excellent Majesty to license me to be a most lowly suitor unto your Highness, which upon my knees in all humble wise I crave.'

This abject appeal might have moved the Queen to have some pity on Katherine, had it not been for the intervention of Francis Newdigate, her mother-in-law's second husband. Without consulting Katherine, he set out to prove the legality of her marriage, and her right to the succession, with the approval of Hertford and his mother, who were anxious to establish the legitimacy of Hertford's sons.

Francis Newdigate enlisted the help of one John Hales, an official at the court. Lame John Hales, Club-foot John Hales, he was called, settled down happily to write a pamphlet entitled 'Declaration of the Succession'. When it was published it caused an uproar in the House of Commons.

Hales was summoned before the Privy Council, where he swore 'by Christ's passion', that he had never dreamed of substituting Lady Katherine for her Majesty, for whom he desired a long and happy reign; his aim was to prevent the succession of Mary Queen of Scots, and in this he had the sympathy of the Protestant half of the country, who wanted no Catholic succession.

Hales was sent to the Fleet prison for six months, and Katherine continued in her banishment. She now became extremely ill and exhausted, and Lord John Grey once more appealed to Cecil, begging him to send one of the Queen's physicians to attend her. He was sure that she was dying of consumption.

Katherine did not die, but Lord John Grey himself died that autumn. She was then sent a few miles away to Ingatestone Hall, the home of Sir William Petre, where the Queen had enjoyed much festivity during her progress to Suffolk. Lady Katherine sunk into apathy. She was weary of life and made no attempt to communicate with anybody, neither her husband, her sister, the Queen, or Cecil.

The little Lady Mary was worried and anxious about her sister, conscious that it was her own intercession with the Queen that had brought about such misery. She was sustained by the kindness of Thomas Keyes. Perhaps kindness was not the right word to use. A warmth had sprung up between them which neither would acknowledge. Sergeant Keyes was as far below Lady Mary socially as he towered above her physically; moreover he was a middle-aged man with grown-up children as old as she was. But Lady Mary was nineteen, time enough to be married. She compared the warm, lovable giant of a man to the cold, unbending stranger to whom she had been betrothed as a child, and who had ruthlessly discarded her when her family fell into disgrace. Sergeant Keyes was no older than him and infinitely more attractive. If she could be betrothed to one, why not the other?

One afternoon they were alone in his apartments, and he brought canary wine and gingerbread to cheer her up. She was sitting on a cushion before his fire, leaning against his knees, and he gently caressed her hair. Impulsively she took his large hand between her own two small ones, and pressed it to her lips. Then somehow she was in his arms and they were kissing each other. This was madness. Perhaps it was so sweet, because it was so dangerous. If the Queen came to hear of it she would be merciless. They drew apart, trembling, confused.

"This cannot be. It is impossible. We must be sensible." Sergeant Keyes was saying, but Lady Mary could only say, repeating it over and over again, "I love you, Tom."

Now they were sweethearts, and in the joy which filled the heart of Lady Mary, she forgot the incongruity of the alliance; forgot all about the difference in their ages and stature and social position. She forgot the plight of her poor unhappy sister, pining for her husband and son, forgot the danger into which she and Tom were running.

It was so usual for her to visit the watergate apartments — she had always done this, that nobody thought twice about it, and perhaps Queen Elizabeth took it for granted that nobody would ever think of wedding her, the plain little dwarf. So they drifted on blissfully throughout the winter and spring into the heat of the summer.

In August, Lettice Knolly's brother Henry was married. They were distantly connected to the Queen, who honoured the nuptials of her kinsman with her presence. In fact, she outshone the bride in the radiance of her countenance and the splendour of her dress. She was very merry and danced with several of her gentlemen but always returned to Leicester, who, like a patient lap-dog was ever at her side. When the Queen withdrew, some of the more boisterous wedding guests adjourned to Master Keyes' apartments, Lady Mary among them. They feasted, danced and romped until nine o'clock at night.

At last there were only half-a-dozen people left, among them Master Keyes' brother Edward. He seemed to be much amused by his brother's affection for the little dwarf, Tom towering over her like some giant.

"And when does *your* wedding take place, brother?" Edward teased. They were all a little intoxicated, and, excited by the mad romping and dancing, ready for anything.

"When will you marry me, sweetheart?" said Thomas Keyes, turning to Lady Mary. "Tonight? Will you wed me tonight?"

"Whenever you say," she answered recklessly.

"We must find a priest," roared Tom. "God's death, but I will be married this night. Meet me here at midnight, good friends, to witness my nuptials with my little Lady Mary."

Thomas Keyes and his brother went off at once to find a priest who would perform the marriage ceremony without asking questions.

A little dazed and fearful, but also excited and happy, Lady Mary went to the Maidens' Bower and pretended to retire for the night, first arranging for her woman to attend her in a chamber off the Bower, that same room once occupied by Lady Jane Seymour. The mother of the maids came to snuff the candles, and to check that no bed was empty. Satisfied, she retired to her own apartment, and

Lady Mary rose as quietly as she was able. The bed pallets were stuffed with straw and it was impossible not to creak and rustle, but if anybody heard her and noted her departure from the dormitory she kept her own counsel. It was not an unusual occurrence for a maid to leave her bed and glide away on business of her own, and no comment was ever made.

Lady Mary's woman was waiting for her, and helped her dress and tired her hair. If the little bride had any misgivings in that quiet room where her sister had plighted her troth to Lord Hertford, she smothered them. She refused to look ahead, to see where this rash act might lead her. Full of happiness and love for her giant, she slipped quietly back, treading softly down the winding staircase she had trod so often to her lover's rooms.

Did he truly mean her to take him seriously, or was it all a drunken joke? Did he really mean to continue with this folly? She hardly believed it until, half-timidly, she pushed open the door of his apartments and found him waiting, a priest by his side. His brother was with him and several other people.

There was only one candle burning, flickering in its sconce, and casting strange shadows on the wall; Thomas, so huge, towered over the priest, who was a little fat old man, wearing a very short gown. It was a strange wedding party, a ludicrous assortment of fat and tall and short; but romance is not the prerogative of the handsome. The love that burned in Lady Mary's stunted body was heightened by gratitude and wonder that it should be returned with such warmth and affection by one so well-proportioned as her beloved Thomas.

Hand-in-hand they stood before the priest. Thomas murmured to his bride that he was a Swiss reformer in exile, but he said the marriage service in English, and according to the Book of Common Prayer. Thomas Keyes slipped on to Lady Mary's finger a gold ring, and they were man and wife. Their friends left them, and Lady Mary went to bed with her husband, where he made love with the most tender affection and she was happy as never before in all her life. Early next morning she quietly returned to the Maidens' Bower.

All was bustle and confusion, for the Queen had made up her mind quite suddenly to go to Windsor. Lady Mary was overjoyed. She knew that the Queen would readily grant her permission to remain at Westminster. It was no secret that Queen Elizabeth only liked to have about her ladies and gentlemen who were comely to look upon. Lady Mary's shortness of stature was an embarrassment to her. She was a nuisance the Queen would rather be without. Lady Katherine, she had disliked, but kept by her side for reasons of security. Now that she was out of the way, there was no reason to be cluttered with her sister. the little dwarf whom nobody was likely to wed.

So off they went, a splendid cavalcade of ladies and gentlemen, leaving the lovers to their happiness. For nine days and nights they dreamed their dream. There was no past and no future, only a sun-filled present. Their minds were drugged with happiness, joy which it was impossible to hide. They were careless of their secret. Life beyond their love did not exist.

On the tenth day after their marriage the Queen returned to Westminster, a raging virago! Too many people had become aware of the romance, and somebody, fearful of being implicated, had divulged the secret.

The Queen's wrath was terrifying. Weeping, on her knees before her, Lady Mary confessed it was true.

"God's death," shrieked the Queen, "I'll have no little bastard Keyes succeeding to my throne."

"No bastards is true," whispered Lady Mary through her tears. "I am truly wed, and none can undo what is done."

"Get out of my sight, hunchback," screamed the Queen. "I will make you sorry you were ever born, let alone wed."

Lady Mary was made over to the Mother of the Maids. She was soundly birched, and kept under lock and key.

After a day of solitary confinement, she was called before the Privy Council to answer their questions regarding the validity of her marriage. Her husband, closely guarded by hallberdiers, was also there to answer for his crime in secretly marrying one so near to the throne. They were questioned and cross-questioned, until there was no doubt in the minds of their inquisitors that they were indeed married. Had their crime been one of fornication no doubt they would have been forgiven; but to have married secretly without the Queen's consent was a heinous offence and the height of folly.

Thomas Keyes was consigned to the Fleet prison, where he was to be kept separate, solitary and silent without communication with anyone. He gave the Lady Mary a look of heart-rending despair before he was marched off out of her life for ever. She never saw him again, for he did not long survive his durance vile.

The Lady Mary's sentence was less severe, but her sorrow as deep. She was kept under lock and key in the care of the Mother of the Maids, until it was certain that she had not become pregnant. She was then dismissed from the court, and put into custody in the charge of one Sir Thomas Hawtrey, at his estate in Buckinghamshire.

All hope of Lady Katherine and Lord Hertford's release from custody was now extinguished by the Lady Mary's imprudence. However, Lord Petre pleaded poverty and begged the Queen to remove Lady Katherine from Ingatestone Hall, as he could no longer afford to keep her. Accordingly, she was moved on, this time to the custody of Sir John Wentworth at Halstead.

Thanks to the benevolence of their step-father, Adrian Stokes, now a prosperous gentleman, both she and Lady Mary were now allowed to receive profits from Grey properties in Warwickshire. He also sent Lady Katherine a spaniel puppy, remembering her love for her pets.

But it was not long before she was passed on again, for Sir John Wentworth, an elderly gentleman, died, and she was consigned to the care of Sir Owen Hopton, at Cockfield Hall in Yoxford, a small Suffolk village.

She was completely isolated, and was told nothing of what had occurred to her sister Mary, nor did she enquire.

She sank into a decline, and it was soon apparent that she was seriously ill. Only her little spaniel could rouse her to any interest, and her affection for him was returned with interest. When she took to her bed, he would lie upon the counterpane at her feet for hour upon hour.

The Queen's physician, Dr Symonds, was sent to her, and visited her regularly, but it was soon apparent to everybody, including herself that she was dying. Her life had become so intolerable to her that she welcomed death with serenity, spending her last night entirely in prayer. At daylight she asked for Sir Owen Hopton.

"Good madam, how do you?" he asked anxiously.

"Even now going to God, Sir Owen," Lady Katherine answered, "even as fast as I can."

She fell silent, then collecting her strength, continued, "And I pray you and the rest that be about me to bear witness that I die a true Christian. And I ask God and all the world forgiveness — and I forgive all the world."

After a little while she continued, "I beseech you, promise me one thing, that you yourself with your own mouth will make this request to the Queen's Majesty, that she will forgive her displeasure towards me, and that she will be good to my children, and not to impute my fault unto them."

Sir Owen promised that he would do as she asked. "And I desire her Highness," Katherine went on, "to be good unto my lord — for I know this my death will be heavy news to him — that her Grace will be so good as to send liberty to glad his sorrowful heart withal."

Then she turned to one of her women, who were gathered about the bed, and said, "Give me the box wherein are my rings."

Summoning all her strength, she opened the box and first drew from it the ring with the pointed diamond. "Here, Sir Owen," she said, "deliver this unto my lord. This is the ring that I received of him when I gave myself to him, and gave him my faith."

After resting a while, she drew out the five-linked ring with Hertford's verse engraved upon it, and said, "Deliver this also to my lord, and pray him, even as I have been to him — as I take God to witness I have been — a true and faithful wife, that he would be a loving father to my children."

Finally she gave him the ring engraved with the death's head and the motto, '*While I live, yours*'.

"This shall be the last token unto my lord that ever I shall send him," she said, adding with a twisted smile, "it is the picture of myself."

She lay quietly with closed eyes in a hushed bedroom, while from across the park the church bell was tolling a peal for each of the twenty-eight years of Lady Katherine's life. She opened her eyes and said, "O Lord, into Thy hands I commend my soul! Lord Jesus, receive my spirit."

Lady Katherine died among strangers, but one mourner she had, who was faithful unto death, for her little spaniel stretched himself over her grave, howling pitifully. No caresses nor even force could detach him from the spot, but he remained there until he died.

Other titles in the
Ulverscroft Large Print Series:

TO FIGHT THE WILD
Rod Ansell and Rachel Percy

Lost in uncharted Australian bush, Rod Ansell survived by hunting and trapping wild animals, improvising shelter and using all the bushman's skills he knew.

COROMANDEL
Pat Barr

India in the 1830s is a hot, uncomfortable place, where the East India Company still rules. Amelia and her new husband find themselves caught up in the animosities which seethe between the old order and the new.

THE SMALL PARTY
Lillian Beckwith

A frightening journey to safety begins for Ruth and her small party as their island is caught up in the dangers of armed insurrection.

FATAL RING OF LIGHT
Helen Eastwood

Katy's brother was supposed to have died in 1897 but a scrawled note in his handwriting showed July 1899. What had happened to him in those two years? Katy was determined to help him.

NIGHT ACTION
Alan Evans

Captain David Brent sails at dead of night to the German occupied Normandy town of St. Jean on a mission which will stretch loyalty and ingenuity to its limits, and beyond.

A MURDER TOO MANY
Elizabeth Ferrars

Many, including the murdered man's widow, believed the wrong man had been convicted. The further murder of a key witness in the earlier case convinced Basnett that the seemingly unrelated deaths were linked.

THE WILDERNESS WALK
Sheila Bishop

Stifling unpleasant memories of a misbegotten romance in Cleave with Lord Francis Aubrey, Lavinia goes on holiday there with her sister. The two women are thrust into a romantic intrigue involving none other than Lord Francis.

THE RELUCTANT GUEST
Rosalind Brett

Ann Calvert went to spend a month on a South African farm with Theo Borland and his sister. They both proved to be different from her first idea of them, and there was Storr Peterson — the most disturbing man she had ever met.

ONE ENCHANTED SUMMER
Anne Tedlock Brooks

A tale of mystery and romance and a girl who found both during one enchanted summer.

CLOUD OVER MALVERTON

Nancy Buckingham

Dulcie soon realises that something is seriously wrong at Malverton, and when violence strikes she is horrified to find herself under suspicion of murder.

AFTER THOUGHTS

Max Bygraves

The Cockney entertainer tells stories of his East End childhood, of his RAF days, and his post-war showbusiness successes and friendships with fellow comedians.

MOONLIGHT AND MARCH ROSES

D. Y. Cameron

Lynn's search to trace a missing girl takes her to Spain, where she meets Clive Hendon. While untangling the situation, she untangles her emotions and decides on her own future.

NURSE ALICE IN LOVE
Theresa Charles

Accepting the post of nurse to little Fernie Sherrod, Alice Everton could not guess at the romance, suspense and danger which lay ahead at the Sherrod's isolated estate.

POIROT INVESTIGATES
Agatha Christie

Two things bind these eleven stories together — the brilliance and uncanny skill of the diminutive Belgian detective, and the stupidity of his Watson-like partner, Captain Hastings.

LET LOOSE THE TIGERS
Josephine Cox

Queenie promised to find the long-lost son of the frail, elderly murderess, Hannah Jason. But her enquiries threatened to unlock the cage where crucial secrets had long been held captive.

THE TWILIGHT MAN
Frank Gruber

Jim Rand lives alone in the California desert awaiting death. Into his hermit existence comes a teenage girl who blows both his past and his brief future wide open.

DOG IN THE DARK
Gerald Hammond

Jim Cunningham breeds and trains gun dogs, and his antagonism towards the devotees of show spaniels earns him many enemies. So when one of them is found murdered, the police are on his doorstep within hours.

THE RED KNIGHT
Geoffrey Moxon

When he finds himself a pawn on the chessboard of international espionage with his family in constant danger, Guy Trent becomes embroiled in moves and countermoves which may mean life or death for Western scientists.

TIGER TIGER
Frank Ryan

A young man involved in drugs is found murdered. This is the first event which will draw Detective Inspector Sandy Woodings into a whirlpool of murder and deceit.

CAROLINE MINUSCULE
Andrew Taylor

Caroline Minuscule, a medieval script, is the first clue to the whereabouts of a cache of diamonds. The search becomes a deadly kind of fairy story in which several murders have an other-worldly quality.

LONG CHAIN OF DEATH
Sarah Wolf

During the Second World War four American teenagers from the same town join the Army together. Forty-two years later, the son of one of the soldiers realises that someone is systematically wiping out the families of the four men.

THE LISTERDALE MYSTERY
Agatha Christie

Twelve short stories ranging from the light-hearted to the macabre, diverse mysteries ingeniously and plausibly contrived and convincingly unravelled.

TO BE LOVED
Lynne Collins

Andrew married the woman he had always loved despite the knowledge that Sarah married him for reasons of her own. So much heartache could have been avoided if only he had known how vital it was to be loved.

ACCUSED NURSE
Jane Converse

Paula found herself accused of a crime which could cost her her job, her nurse's reputation, and even the man she loved, unless the truth came to light.

BUTTERFLY MONTANE
Dorothy Cork

Parma had come to New Guinea to marry Alec Rivers, but she found him completely disinterested and that overbearing Pierce Adams getting entirely the wrong idea about her.

HONOURABLE FRIENDS
Janet Daley

Priscilla Burford is happily married when she meets Junior Environment Minister Alistair Thurston. Inevitably, sexual obsession and political necessity collide.

WANDERING MINSTRELS
Mary Delorme

Stella Wade's career as a concert pianist might have been ruined by the rudeness of a famous conductor, so it seemed to her agent and benefactor. Even Sir Nicholas fails to see the possibilities when John Tallis falls deeply in love with Stella.

CHATEAU OF FLOWERS
Margaret Rome

Alain, Comte de Treville needed a wife to look after him, and Fleur went into marriage on a business basis only, hoping that eventually he would come to trust and care for her.

CRISS-CROSS
Alan Scholefield

As her ex-husband had succeeded in kidnapping their young daughter once, Jane was determined to take her safely back to England. But all too soon Jane is caught up in a new web of intrigue.

DEAD BY MORNING
Dorothy Simpson

Leo Martindale's body was discovered outside the gates of his ancestral home. Is it, as Inspector Thanet begins to suspect, murder?